Witch Summer Night's Cream

Bewitched by Chocolate Mysteries

Book Three

H.Y. Hanna

ISBN-13: 978-0-9954012-80

CONTENTS

CHAPTER ONE

"That creepy chap is here again."

Caitlyn Le Fey glanced up from where she was carefully ladling some rich, hot chocolate into an earthenware mug and looked at the teenage girl across the counter. Though already eighteen, Evie was still gangly-limbed and pimply-faced, with an awkward manner that reminded Caitlyn of a clumsy colt, and an untidy halo of frizzy red hair which defied all attempts to tame it. It was more of a carroty-red—not the deep crimson of Caitlyn's own hair—but it was the one thing which instantly and obviously connected the two girls, and reminded Caitlyn that they were cousins.

Cousins. Caitlyn smiled as she repeated the word in her mind. It still seemed a bit surreal sometimes. When she had come to England over a month ago to search for her real family, the last thing she had expected was to find her roots here in the tiny village of Tillyhenge, deep in the Cotswolds countryside. And not only had she found a grandmother, an aunt, and a cousin to claim for her very own, she'd discovered that they were no ordinary grandmother, aunt, and cousin either.

They were witches. And Caitlyn was one of them.

It had taken her a while to come to terms with that, to tell the truth. After all, unlike her other, adoptive cousin, Pomona—who had grown up in Hollywood and embraced every New Age fad and occult belief—Caitlyn had never believed in magic. She had always scoffed at things like divination and witchcraft, fairies and spells, and dismissed legends and myths as silly stories. Until she had arrived in Tillyhenge, that is. It had been a shock to discover that magic was real—and that *she* could harness it to do her bidding.

Well, a little bit, anyway.

Caitlyn dropped her gaze to the ladle, which she had just returned to the small cauldron behind the counter. Casting a furtive glance around, she waved her fingers surreptitiously over the long silver handle. The ladle quivered, then slowly began gliding around the cauldron in a clockwise direction, stirring the hot chocolate by itself. Caitlyn felt an involuntary smile of delight tug her lips.

Of course, enchanting a ladle was beginner's level stuff. After a week of daily training with the

Widow Mags, her formidable grandmother, she should have really been focusing on mastering more advanced skills. But it was all still such a novelty that Caitlyn found herself delighted in being able to perform even the smallest feats of magic. *Besides, such small feats are about the only thing I* can *do with reliability,* she thought ruefully. So far, despite repeated attempts and trying very hard, she still hadn't been able to master the more advanced skills and spells—such as turning something into chocolate and bringing chocolate creations to life.

"Caitlyn, did you hear what I said?"

Caitlyn snapped out of her thoughts and looked up. "Sorry, Evie... um... who's creepy?"

"Him." Evie jerked her chin across the room to a man sitting at one of the tables on the other side of the chocolate store.

Caitlyn followed the direction of her cousin's gaze and narrowed her eyes thoughtfully. "Creepy" wasn't exactly the word she would have chosen. She saw a thin old man in a shabby tweed jacket, with grey tufty hair that seemed to be sprouting from his ears, as well as his head and eyebrows, and spectacles perched on the end of his nose. His wrinkled face was puckered in concentration as he pored over a stack of books open on the table in front of him and he sipped absent-mindedly from a cup of hot chocolate at his elbow.

"Why do you think he's creepy?" she asked.

"Well, he's been coming every day for the past

three days. I've seen him every afternoon when I've come here after school. And he always sits in that corner. That's a bit weird, don't you think?"

Caitlyn had to admit that this was true. *Bewitched by Chocolate* wasn't exactly what you'd call a "bustling" shop and repeat customers were rare. Partly because most of the people who ventured in were casual tourists who happened to stop in the village whilst touring the Cotswolds. In fact, it was a miracle that they even found the chocolate shop in the first place, tucked as it was at the back of the village, away from the main activity near the village green.

Of course, they could have had regular visitors in the local residents, but most of the villagers refused to set foot in the shop. They were frightened of the Widow Mags—the strange old woman who owned the store—and the chocolates, which melted on your tongue and tasted so amazing that everyone whispered: they *had* to have been bewitched by dark magic.

Caitlyn felt a familiar mixture of frustration and exasperation at the thought of the villagers' fearful attitudes. It was ridiculous—to be scared of something and think it's evil, just because it tasted so mouth-wateringly good!

Still, all of this meant that Evie was right—it was hard enough to get a customer to step into the shop in the first place, never mind come back for three days in a row. She looked curiously again at the elderly gentleman. Perhaps he was staying in the village? That would explain his daily reappearance. Though wouldn't she have heard if there was a stranger staying in Tillyhenge? The village was tiny, with only a smattering of shops and a pub on one side of the village green, and news travelled like wildfire on the local grapevine. *Well, perhaps not to me,* Caitlyn thought wryly. Her association with the Widow Mags meant that most of the villagers avoided her too and certainly didn't include her in their inner gossip circles.

"Maybe he just really likes chocolates," she said to Evie with a shrug. "It's not a crime to return to the same shop every day and a lot of people have a 'favourite seat'. As long as he's a paying customer." She grinned.

"Yes, but it's not just that. He keeps asking me all these odd questions too—about magic and fairies and enchanted forests..."

"Well, Tillyhenge *does* have a bit of a reputation as a village with magical associations, remember? Especially because of the stone circle nearby," Caitlyn reminded her. "Everyone thinks this place is steeped in witchcraft and you know how much it fascinates the tourists. Maybe it's just vulgar curiosity—"

Evie shook her head. "No. This is different. It's not like when tourists ask about local myths and legends—he seems to know all the legends himself already! It's more as if he's... he's searching for answers to something."

Caitlyn thought for a moment. Tillyhenge had been mentioned a lot in the news and on social media recently. Well, when you had stories circulating about sinister murders and chocolate wart curses, a place was bound to gain some notoriety.

"Maybe he's a journalist, sniffing around for a scoop?" She looked at the younger girl. "You didn't tell him you're a witch, did you?"

"No, of course not!" said Evie. "He asked me what Mum did and I told him she's a herbalist, which is sort of true." She paused, then muttered, "I don't know why I bother, though. I mean, everyone in the village is probably jumping to tell him nasty stuff about us anyway. They're always talking behind my back."

Caitlyn eyed the younger girl with surprise. Evie was normally so sweet and cheerful—this bitterness was unlike her.

"Have you been getting teased at school?" she asked gently.

Evie shrugged unconvincingly. "It's my last year anyway."

Caitlyn hesitated. She had been home-schooled herself and so had been spared a lot of the usual high school anguish, but she had heard enough horror stories to know how tough it could be, especially if you were "different".

"You mustn't let them get to you, you know.

They're probably just jealous—I'm sure lots of girls would secretly love to be a witch."

"What's the point of being a witch when you're not even allowed to use magic half the time?" asked Evie petulantly.

Before Caitlyn could answer, two tourists came up to the counter. Hastily, Caitlyn flicked her fingers at the enchanted ladle to stop it stirring and turned to the two ladies.

"Can we have more of those strawberries with the chocolate sauce?" they asked eagerly.

"More?" Caitlyn looked at them askance. "Um... you've already had two dozen. Are you sure you should be having more?"

They bobbed their heads, barely listening to her, their eyes riveted on the beautifully-arranged pyramid of juicy red strawberries standing on the counter. Each strawberry had been drizzled with a rich chocolate sauce which had dried into a glossy dark coat of crisp chocolate lattice around the fruit.

"Uh... okay..." Caitlyn gave them another doubtful look, then carefully plucked a dozen strawberries off the pyramid. She had barely had time to place them on a plate before the two ladies had shoved some money at her, grabbed the plate, and started stuffing the juicy, chocolate-covered berries in their mouths.

"What's going on with the strawberries?" Caitlyn asked Evie in an undertone as the two ladies moved away. "People have been coming back all day, asking to buy more. I know they've always been very popular but this is a bit crazy."

"I think it's the new chocolate sauce Grandma made," said Evie. "I heard her talking to Mum about it. She's added something special to it and—"

She broke off suddenly, her eyes widening with dismay as she stared at the shop doorway. Caitlyn turned and saw a girl of about Evie's age step into the store. She had dark brown hair with a blunt fringe, cut in a trendy style, and a superficial prettiness, which was marred by the insolent expression on her face. She sauntered over to the counter, swinging a pink tote bag and lazily chewing on a piece of gum.

"Hiya Evie…"

"Uh… H-h-hi, Mandy…" Evie stammered, backing away slightly.

The other girl leaned against the counter and smirked. "Not peddling potions over at your mum's freaky herbal shop today?"

Evie flushed and looked down.

Mandy laughed. Then she peered at Evie with fake concern. "Bloody hell, that's a huge zit on your nose, Evie. *Eeuww…* and it's a whitehead! Gross!"

Evie clamped a hand over her nose, mortified. "It's… it just came up this morning," she mumbled.

Mandy snapped her fingers. "Oh, but you're a witch, right? How come you've still got a face full of spots? Can't you conjure up a spell to get rid of your pimples?" She giggled. "Or is your acne too disgusting, even for witchcraft?"

Evie was scarlet now and blinking rapidly, as if holding back tears. Caitlyn felt a surge of anger. She knew girls like Mandy; they were the same all over the world: the "popular" girls, the prom queens and darlings of cheerleading teams, always effortlessly pretty and graceful, with adoring groupies and besotted boys following in their wake—and always picking on those less fortunate. Girls like Evie with her frizzy hair and bad complexion.

"Did you want to buy something?" she asked curtly.

Mandy looked at the chocolate truffles beneath the glass counter and gave a sniff. "Dunno. Are these safe to eat?"

Caitlyn glanced around the store. There were several tourists browsing and she didn't want to make a scene in front of them, otherwise she would have dearly loved to give Mandy a piece of her mind.

"Yes, they're fine," she said through gritted teeth.

"I'll take some of those, then," said Mandy, pointing to the display of milk chocolate pralines with peanut butter and roasted hazelnuts. "And those too," she added, moving her finger to the rows of vanilla mocha ganache covered with crisp, dark chocolate.

Caitlyn grabbed the tongs and quickly filled up a small box, hoping to get rid of the girl as soon as possible. But as she handed the chocolates across the counter, another figure stepped through the front doorway. It was a boy—well, a young man, really—of eighteen, with an open, good-looking face and a thatch of sun-streaked blond hair, which gave him a bit of a "surfer" vibe. He had that lanky, angular look of boys on the verge of manhood, with an Adam's apple bobbing prominently in his throat and hands that looked slightly too big for his body, but you could see the hint of the handsome man he would become one day, once he grew into his tall frame.

It was Chris Bottom, Caitlyn realised, a local boy who had recently started a summer job at nearby Huntingdon Manor, lending a helping hand wherever he was needed. His lanky figure sitting astride one of the Manor's quad bikes had become a familiar sight around the village. As he walked in, Evie gave a breathless squeak and turned even brighter red, if that was possible. Mandy glanced at her and a malicious smile touched her lips.

"Ooh, I forgot—you've got a crush on Chris, haven't you, Evie?" she said in a loud stage whisper. She smacked her lips, making mock kissing sounds, and giggled. "Mel told me she saw you writing 'Mrs Evie Bottom' in your notebook in Economics class... aww, isn't that sweet?"

Evie made a choked sound in her throat, her eyes darting wildly from Mandy to Chris, who was still out of earshot, but who would arrive at the counter any moment. She put a frantic hand up to her frizzy hair, trying to tuck it behind her ears.

Mandy looked her up and down contemptuously and said with a snigger, "Better start brewing a love potion, Evie, because that's the only way someone like Chris would ever look at *you*!"

Evie's hands clenched around the handle of the mug she was holding, her knuckles so white that Caitlyn thought she might crack the ceramic. Her chest heaved and she stared at Mandy with a mixture of fear and hatred.

Mandy laughed again, unconcerned, then turned to Chris as he arrived at the counter. She smoothed down her sundress and said, giving him a flirtatious smile, "Hiya, Chris."

"Hi, Mandy," he said, blushing slightly. He looked expectantly at Evie and said, "Um... I'm here to pick up those chocolate samples for the Manor?"

Evie stared at him, opening and closing her mouth, like a goldfish gasping its last breath, but no sound came out. Mandy sniggered loudly again. There was a long silence as Chris continued looking at Evie, his easy smile fading into an expression of bewilderment.

Hastily, Caitlyn stepped in and said, "Er... maybe I can help, Chris. Which chocolates are these?"

The boy turned to her gratefully. "They're for Lisa—you know, the Events Coordinator up at the Manor. She reckons it'd be cool to serve chocolates with the 'Afternoon Tea' at the end of the official tour. And, like, if people stay over at the Manor—they can have chocolates in their rooms or on their beds—like in those posh hotels, y'know? And for the weddings and conferences and other events—" He broke off suddenly and sneezed a couple of times. "Sorry." He sniffed. "Hay fever."

"Here." Caitlyn handed him some napkins and waited politely as he blew his nose.

"Thanks." He sniffed again, then continued. "Anyway, Lisa wants the Widow Mags to make some special chocolates—just for the Manor—and then she'll put some fancy paper around 'em, paper that's printed with the Huntingdon Manor coat of arms." He rubbed his hands enthusiastically. "James—I mean, Lord Fitzroy—thought it was a cracking idea! He said the Widow Mags can become our supplier and we can tell the guests about the shop here too. Only, he and Lisa weren't sure which flavours to have, so the Widow Mags said she'd make a few samples and they could choose."

"Ah." Caitlyn looked under the counter and spied a cardboard box which had been set aside. She picked it up and opened it to see a jumble of chocolate truffles in a variety of flavours. "This must be it."

"Ta," said Chris, reaching for the box.

"Chris..." Mandy purred. "Have you finished your economics project yet?"

"Yeah, I finished it last week."

"Oh, lucky you..." Mandy pouted. "I've still got

half of it to do." She sidled closer to him and put a hand on his arm. "You're so good with numbers, Chris... Could you help me?"

Chris's face reddened. "Uh... sure."

"You're heading back to the Manor now, right?" she asked, giving him a dazzling smile. "My house is on the way. We can stop off and I can show you what I've done so far."

She started to turn away but Caitlyn stopped her, pointing to the box of chocolates that Mandy had tucked into her tote bag.

"You haven't paid for your chocolates."

A look of chagrin and annoyance crossed the girl's face, but she gave a forced laugh. "Oh... I completely forgot."

That might have been true but Caitlyn had seen the way Mandy had deliberately slipped the box into her bag when she thought nobody was looking. Caitlyn said nothing, waiting pointedly until the girl had tossed some money down on the counter with bad grace. Mandy scowled, then she darted a look at Evie, who was still standing, tongue-tied, and a spiteful gleam came into her eyes.

"Chris..." she cooed. "Can I ride with you? I've been walking all over today and my feet are killing me!" She raised a bare leg and showed off her shapely calf.

Chris looked doubtful. "I've only got my normal bike with me—not the quad bike."

"Oh, that's all right!" said Mandy. "I can just

perch on the handlebars. I've always wanted to do that—it looks so romantic!" She glanced sideways at Evie again, a smile curling the corners of her mouth.

"Uh... okay," said Chris, rubbing the back of his neck and breaking into a sheepish grin.

He allowed himself to be dragged outside and they saw him putting his hands awkwardly around Mandy's waist to help steady her, as she climbed, giggling, onto the handlebars of his bicycle. Caitlyn glanced at Evie and her heart contracted at the anguish she saw on her cousin's face. It was cruel, what Mandy was doing—like someone dangling a delicious morsel of food in front of a starving person, then purposefully eating it themselves. She wanted to say something but didn't know what to say. Instead, they both watched silently as Chris climbed astride the bike and he and Mandy wobbled off together down the lane, out of sight. The sound of Mandy's shrieking laughter drifted back to them.

"Evie?" Caitlyn said gently, touching her arm.

Evie gave a start, then turned around, her face flushed and her eyes suspiciously bright.

"I hate her! I HATE HER!" she cried, her voice shrill with emotion. "I... I wish Mandy Harper would drop dead!"

CHAPTER TWO

An awkward silence descended in the chocolate shop as the remaining customers all turned around to stare. Caitlyn gave them a wan smile, then turned back to Evie and said in a low, urgent voice:

"Evie, you mustn't let Mandy get to you! She was mad at me for making her pay for those chocolates so she took it out by tormenting you. Besides, I could see that she was trying to push your buttons the moment she stepped in the shop. People like that make themselves feel good by putting others down—"

"But it's true what she said," Evie whispered, hanging her head. "It's true that Chris Bottom would never look at me unless I had a love potion."

"That's... that's not true," Caitlyn protested.

She looked at the younger girl helplessly, wishing

she knew what to say to bolster Evie's confidence. But to be honest, confidence had never been her strong suit. If anything, Caitlyn could relate to Evie's feelings of inferiority only too well. She was used to being the ugly duckling in her glamorous showbiz family. Her late adoptive mother, Barbara Le Fey, had been a renowned American singer with a sultry voice and easy natural charm; her aunt—Barbara's sister—was a Hollywood actress famous for her seductive looks and kooky personality; and her cousin, Pomona, was the classic celebrity princess: gorgeous, confident, and at home in the spotlight.

Caitlyn wished some of their easy assurance had rubbed off on her, but despite growing up surrounded by all these examples of beauty and charisma, she had remained shy and homely, self-conscious about her big hips and nervous about drawing attention to herself.

She pushed these thoughts aside now as she reminded herself that she was The Older Person here (even if it was only by four years). In fact, in a way, it was nice to feel like the "older and wiser one" for once. She had always felt so gawky and naïve compared to Pomona, who—despite being the same age—was always more glamorous and sophisticated. This was the first time that Caitlyn had someone to "care for", and she found herself feeling very protective towards Evie. She realised that she should give the younger girl some words of wisdom and try to bolster her self-esteem. That's what Pomona would do if she was here.

Caitlyn cleared her throat. "I'm sure that if Chris... uh... got to know you better and... um... well, it's not all about the perfect hair and figure, you know... um... you want to be loved for your inner beauty too... and... um—" she floundered.

Then she realised that Evie wasn't even listening. The girl had her head down, muttering to herself.

"... so what? I *could* do it... it would be so easy... he wouldn't even know and then—"

"Evie?" Caitlyn said uneasily. "What are you talking about?"

The other girl blinked. "About... about making a love potion," she said in a defiant tone.

"A love potion?" Caitlyn gave a sceptical laugh.

Evie frowned. "What's so funny? I'm serious! And I'll bet it's easy! It's like making up any kind of potion, really—you just need to have the right ingredients and know the spell for combining them. Then it works like a dream." She gestured to the chocolate-covered strawberries. "Why do you think everyone's been going bonkers for the strawberries?"

Caitlyn stared at her, then at the pyramid of red fruit, then back to Evie again. "What do you mean?"

"I told you—Grandma added something special to the chocolate sauce. It makes anything the sauce is poured on absolutely delicious and people can't get enough of it." Evie nodded. "I'm sure she added some kind of love potion to the chocolate sauce recipe."

"Love potion?" Caitlyn said again, still having trouble wrapping her mind around the concept. It was one thing to accept that magic did exist, but love potions seemed to be something from the realm of movies and fairy tales. "You mean... it really works? Really makes people fall in love? But what's in it?"

"I don't know," said Evie. "I heard her say it's something which only flowers at this time of the year... you know, around Midsummer's Eve."

A sound next to them made them suddenly realise that they weren't alone. There was a man standing next to the counter—the "creepy" gentleman Evie had been talking about earlier.

"I beg your pardon... I came over for another cup of hot chocolate and I couldn't help overhearing your conversation..." He peered at them through his spectacles and said breathlessly, "Did I hear you say Midsummer's Eve? And a... a love potion?"

Evie hesitated, giving Caitlyn a guilty look. The last thing she should have been doing was revealing the Widow Mags's secret recipes to the public. "Well, um... I might have heard wrong," she said quickly, trying to backtrack. "I mean, there aren't really any love potions, of course—"

"Oh, but there are!" cried the old man. "In fact, there is a very famous love potion that's associated with Midsummer's Eve! Shakespeare himself wrote about it—ah, forgive me. I haven't introduced myself. I'm Professor Ruskin." He beamed at them. "I'm a Shakespearean scholar, you see, with a particular interest in *A Midsummer Night's Dream.* In fact, I have devoted my life to studying that play and I am convinced that Shakespeare based his story on fact!"

"Er... on *fact*?" Caitlyn gave him an uncertain look. "The play is about a bunch of fairies—"

"Oh, but fairies are real! It's just that most of us can't see them!" insisted Professor Ruskin.

Oh dear, Caitlyn thought. The poor old thing was obviously completely cuckoo. He was babbling on, his spectacles glinting as he bobbed his head.

"...why I've come to Tillyhenge. I'm well aware of the reputation of this village and its connections to witchcraft and magic—and what better time to study the source of the story than during the summer solstice! I'm sure I'll find the proof I need to support my theories—" He broke off as he saw the two girls looking at him in bewilderment. "Ah, forgive me, my dears... I have not told you my grand hypothesis yet, have I? You see, I believe that Shakespeare was inspired by a real-life enchanted forest. Naturally, one would think of the Forest of Arden, the ancient forest which once stood near Shakespeare's home town of Stratford-upon-Avon. But I posit—" he waved a finger excitedly, "—I posit that the forest which inspired *A Midsummer Night's Dream* is none other than the one behind this village!"

"You may wonder how I came to this conclusion," he continued, ignoring Caitlyn's and Evie's befuddled expressions. "I devoted several months to the research of 'enchanted forests' throughout Great Britain—hours spent in the Bodleian Library in Oxford, examining ancient texts—but I was rewarded for my efforts! There are numerous woods which lay claim to the 'enchanted' title, you see, but I have arrived at a definitive answer. It is remarkably simple, really, once one knows where to look. Indeed, Shakespeare laid out all the clues in his own play!"

"He… he did?" said Caitlyn.

Professor Ruskin nodded eagerly. "Yes, yes. There is a passage which mentions cowslips in Act 2, Scene 1. '*And hang a pearl in every cowslip's ear*'."

"Cowslips?" Caitlyn said, completely lost now.

"They're small yellow flowers which grow wild in the meadows," Evie spoke up. "They bloom in early spring. You can make wine from the flowers and use the roots in herbal remedies, to treat things like rheumatism. Mum uses it in several of her concoctions."

"And the cowslips of the Cotswolds are particularly renowned for their beauty," said the professor. "So you see, it all fits! The village of Tillyhenge, deep in the countryside famous for its cowslips, with an ancient forest at its back that's known to have connections to magic... an 'enchanted' forest..." He whirled towards Evie, his eyes feverishly bright. "And now I hear a local talking about a love potion! That can be none other than the same potion used by Puck the fairy in the play. Oh, my dear—I had dreamt that such a potion could exist and now I find that it is true!" He gripped her arm, his fingers digging into her skin and making Evie wince. "Do you have it here? Can you show it to me?"

"N-n-no," said Evie, trying to pull her arm out of his grasp. "I... the potion isn't real!"

"But I heard you talk about it just now!" the professor insisted. "You said your grandmother—the dear lady who owns this chocolate shop—used it herself in her chocolate sauce recipe."

"I... I was joking," stammered Evie. "It's not... there isn't any love potion."

Professor Ruskin frowned, his face darkening. "You are lying to me," he said, advancing towards her.

"N-no, I'm not," said Evie, backing away. "I honestly don't know... I was making it up..." She shifted around the counter, trying to put it between herself and the old man, but he followed her.

"You must tell me the truth!" Professor Ruskin pleaded. "This is my life's work! This is—*aarrgh*!"

Evie's hand, which had been groping behind her, found the door behind the counter which led to the rooms at the rear of the cottage. She pushed it open, but before she could step through, a tiny ball of black fur shot out, colliding with the old man's ankles. He cried out and pitched forwards, sprawling on the floor in a tangle of bony legs and arms.

"Oh, I'm so sorry," cried Evie, kneeling down to help him.

"Nibs!" shouted Caitlyn, diving to grab the kitten, but the little cat evaded her grasp and darted between her legs, causing Caitlyn to stumble and almost fall over herself.

"*Meew!*" said the kitten cheekily, and he scampered out into the front of the shop. The tourists turned and saw him.

"Oh! Look! A baby kitty! How adorable!" cooed one woman, tugging at her husband's sleeve.

"Crikey! Something just tripped me... hey, is that a cat?"

"Mummy, look, there's a cat!" A little boy pointed.

Two French women whirled around. "*Ah! Un chat! Comme il est mignon!*"

"NIBS!" Caitlyn shouted above the commotion. "Nibs, come back here!"

"*Meew*!" squeaked the kitten, running in circles around the tourists.

Caitlyn lunged for him and missed, but her move had forced him to double back towards the counter. He scampered past Evie and Professor Ruskin, who was still sitting on the floor, slightly dazed, and ran behind the counter. Caitlyn chased after him but Nibs dodged her again, this time diving through the partially open door back into the rear of the cottage. Panting, Caitlyn rushed through the door as well and into the kitchen. The kitten scrambled onto one of the chairs at the wooden table and turned around to face her, his eyes bright with mischief.

"Nibs, you—" Caitlyn broke off as she suddenly realised that there was somebody else in the kitchen.

A man was standing frozen in the doorway of the old pantry, now converted to a stillroom, and he had a guilty expression on his face.

"Who are you?" Caitlyn demanded. "What are you doing here?"

CHAPTER THREE

The man hastily stepped out of the stillroom and came towards Caitlyn.

"Dennis Kirby," he said, holding a hand out to her. "I have an appointment to see the Widow Mags."

Caitlyn frowned. He looked vaguely familiar—had she met him before? That sandy hair, combed over to one side, the narrow face with those calculating brown eyes and limp moustache... Then she remembered. He had been here earlier in the week: a local businessman of some kind, come to see the Widow Mags with an offer. He had been closeted with the old witch in the kitchen for a long time. Caitlyn didn't know what they had talked about but, whatever it was, it obviously hadn't gone as Kirby had planned. He'd left with his mouth set in an ugly line and his face like thunder.

Today, however, his face was plastered with an oily smile. Caitlyn didn't take the hand he offered. Instead, she asked again:

"What are you doing in the kitchen?"

"I was waiting for the Widow Mags," he said smoothly. "I arrived a bit early and found the back door unlocked, so I thought I'd wait in here."

Caitlyn glanced at the back door, which was slightly ajar, and had to admit that he could have been telling the truth. The Widow Mags and Bertha, Evie's mother, had gone out to the forest earlier to gather wild herbs, and they could well have left the door unlocked. Tillyhenge was still the sort of place where most people knew everyone else and hardly anyone locked their doors in the daytime.

Still, she didn't trust him. "You weren't just waiting, though—you were snooping around in the stillroom," she pointed out.

The man gave her an innocent look. "The stillroom? What's that? I was... uh... looking for the toilet, actually."

A toilet in the kitchen? Yeah, right. It was obvious that he was lying. And she had the feeling that Dennis Kirby knew exactly what a stillroom was, although he was certainly putting on a good act. She wondered what he had been searching for. She knew that the Widow Mags distilled her tonics, tinctures, and cordials, and stored her dry herbs and other ingredients in the stillroom. Before she could question him further, however, they heard the sound of voices approaching the back door and, a minute later, two women stepped into the kitchen.

One was a plump, middle-aged, motherly figure clad in a voluminous purple kaftan, with a large wicker basket over one arm, filled with flowers, grasses, and herbs. Aunt Bertha. She had frizzy red hair just like Evie's and a kindly face with a gentle smile. She put her basket on the counter and bent down to pat Nibs, who had scampered over to her, his little tail up in the air.

The other was an old woman with a hunched back, hands gnarled with arthritis, fierce, flashing eyes, and a large hooked nose—the classic image of the "witch" seen in so many books and movies. It was easy to see why the Widow Mags instilled fear and suspicion in the villagers. Not that her grandmother's manner helped matters, Caitlyn reflected ruefully. Blunt and cantankerous, the Widow Mags certainly didn't make it easy to like her.

"Widow Mags!" said Dennis Kirby, hurrying forwards with his hand thrust out. "How nice to see you again! I suppose you've been out enjoying the fine weather? A remarkably good summer we're having, isn't it? I was just—"

"What do you want?" the old woman snapped.

Kirby faltered to a stop, then his expression hardened and he said, "Have you thought about my offer?"

"I have. And the answer is still no."

"What do you mean, 'no'? I'm offering you good money!" Kirby said angrily. "Are you holding out for more? Is that it? Well, I'm telling you, you won't get another penny from me so don't think you can—"

"I told you, it's not about the money."

He gave a patronising laugh. "Of course it's about the money. It's always about the money. I've negotiated with much tougher customers than you, Widow Mags, so don't think you can get me to raise my offer by digging your heels in." He leaned forwards and changed his voice to a cajoling tone. "Come on, I'm making you a good offer here—a more than generous offer. And with my factory manufacturing the product, you could have the chance to get your chocolate sauce into every household in England! Look, I'll even put your name on the label—how's that? 'The Widow Mags's Special Chocolate Sauce'... got a nice ring, eh?" He gave her a winsome smile. "All you have to do is tell me the recipe. In fact, I don't even need the whole recipe. I've worked out most of it already—it's just this last ingredient. What is it? What makes it so that everyone can't get enough of your chocolate sauce?"

His tone became more urgent as the Widow Mags didn't respond. "All right, I'll raise the money. Double. There. I'll pay you *double* what I was offering. All you have to do is tell me the secret ingredient."

The Widow Mags looked at him impatiently. "I told you, I'm not interested in your money."

Dennis Kirby flushed with frustration. "I'm not giving up, you know," he blustered. "I'll be back here next week—and the week after—"

"You'd be wasting your time," said the Widow Mags. "The answer will still be no."

"Why you—!" He broke off as Nibs scampered up to him with an expression of curiosity on his whiskered face.

"*Meew?*" said the kitten.

"Get away from me!" snarled Kirby, making a kicking motion with his foot. "Filthy little beast!"

Bertha gasped in outrage, scooping up Nibs quickly. "He's just a baby."

The businessman gave her another disgusted look; then, clenching his fists, he turned and stormed out of the kitchen.

Widow Mags snorted "Good riddance!" and hobbled out to the shop at the front. Caitlyn hastily followed as she remembered with a guilty pang that she had left Evie outside on her own. She was relieved to find that the tourists had calmed down and that Professor Ruskin—together with his mad theories—had left for the day. They closed the chocolate shop soon after and retired to the back of the cottage, where Bertha rustled up a simple dinner of succulent honey-glazed ham and English mustard, fresh asparagus and watercress salad, home-made relishes and a large loaf of crusty country bread, all finished off with a delicious gooseberry tart.

As they were licking the last of the creamy tart from their dessert spoons, Evie spoke up:

"Grandma, will you make more of the chocolate sauce?"

The Widow Mags looked at her in surprise. "There's still some left, isn't there?"

"Not much. All the chocolate-drizzled strawberries sold out and everyone was asking for more. They even wanted chocolate sauce on their cakes and fudge. And they were buying the jars to take home too."

The Widow Mags nodded. "I'll make some more first thing in the morning,"

"Um... well, I really wanted to watch how you do it," said Evie quickly.

The old woman looked at her in slight surprise—Evie had never shown much interest in chocolate-making before— then she nodded again and lifted Nibs from her lap. The little kitten had curled up in one of his favourite positions—on the Widow Mags's lap, under the table—and blinked sleepily now, mewing in protest as she rose and gently deposited him on her chair. Then she gathered a few ingredients and cleared a space at the other end of the long, wooden table.

The two girls watched, fascinated, as she placed chunks of gourmet dark chocolate together with fresh cream into a deep copper pot, which she heated above a cauldron of simmering water until the chocolate melted into the cream in beautiful, dark swirls. Then she added a knob of butter, a generous helping of cocoa powder, some sugar, a pinch of salt, and a dash of vanilla, stirring continuously until the dark, molten mixture became thick and glossy.

Caitlyn could feel her mouth beginning to water as the heady fragrance of rich, decadent chocolate filled the kitchen. When the Widow Mags finally lifted the pot off the fire and brought it to the table, she couldn't resist reaching out a finger towards the dribble of chocolate sauce on the side of the pot.

"Wait... there is one more ingredient," said the Widow Mags.

Evie watched avidly as the old woman walked to the stillroom and paused just inside the doorway. A locked cupboard was mounted high on the wall. The Widow Mags waved a hand in front of the cabinet door and muttered: "*Aperio!*" The door swung open and Caitlyn saw various miniature bottles and vials, each with paper labels tied to strings around their necks. The Widow Mags lifted a small glass vial off the top shelf and returned to the table.

"Is that... Grandma, is that the love potion?" asked Evie breathlessly, staring at the vial.

Bertha answered, "Yes. I helped to brew it—from the juice of the 'love-in-idleness' flower."

Caitlyn gave a disbelieving laugh. "What? The same flower as in *A Midsummer Night's Dream*? But that's... that's just something Shakespeare made up!"

The Widow Mags raised an eyebrow. "Is it?"

"Are you telling me that the story is true?" said Caitlyn incredulously. "That Cupid really shot an arrow which missed its target and landed on a purple flower instead—and the juice from that flower can make people fall in love?"

Bertha chuckled. "As to that, we don't know. The truth has been lost in the mists of time. But there really is a flower called 'love-in-idleness'—it's more commonly known as the wild pansy."

"But... pansies grow everywhere," Caitlyn protested. "Surely if its juice could be used as a love potion, people would have realised by now."

"Ah, but the juice for the potion doesn't just come from any wild pansy," said Bertha. "It must be extracted from a particular variety that only blooms a few days before Midsummer's Eve. It takes great skill to recognise those special flowers—skills which only witches possess."

She reached across and picked up the vial, holding it up to the light. Caitlyn saw that it was a third full with some kind of clear liquid.

"This potion is made up of juice extracted from flowers we harvested last summer. Mother and I have been searching for the last few days but we haven't found any 'love-in-idleness' blooms yet." Bertha sighed. "With Midsummer's Eve just two days away, time is running out. If we don't pick new flowers this year, I won't be able to make a fresh batch of the potion and this—" she gave the vial a little shake, "—will have to last us until next summer."

The Widow Mags took the vial and pulled out the stopper. "Fortunately, you only need a tiny bit for this recipe," she said with a smile as she tipped the vial over the pot of chocolate sauce and carefully poured out one drop.

There was a hiss and a cloud of purple steam rose from the pot. The Widow Mags stirred the chocolate sauce and chanted something softly under her breath—so softly that Caitlyn couldn't hear the words. It must have been an incantation of some kind, however, because the chocolate sauce began to glimmer. A soft moonlight glow rose from the pot, then faded slowly. The Widow Mags dabbed a finger against the side of the pot, lifting up some of the rich chocolate sauce. She licked her finger, then nodded.

"I think that'll do."

Picking up the vial, she sealed it again and returned it to the stillroom cupboard. Caitlyn saw Evie watching the Widow Mags wistfully. Then a sound outside the kitchen window caught her attention. She glanced across, frowning. Had she imagined it? It had sounded almost like a thump followed by a muffled curse... She crossed swiftly to the open window and looked out, half-expecting to see someone crouched there.

There was no one. And yet...

Caitlyn leaned out and strained her eyes to see in the gathering darkness. It was nearly ten but the sun set late in June and there was still enough twilight, as well as the glow from the rising moon, to make out faint shapes: the vegetables, flowers, and herbs growing in the cottage garden, the silhouette of the trees standing beyond, the gentle slope of the hill behind the cottage, rising up to the horizon, with the forest sweeping up over one side, like a dark green blanket covering half the hill. And there—just at the edge of the forest beside the cottage—was that a figure? Caitlyn peered harder but couldn't make out what it was before it disappeared through the trees.

"Caitlyn?"

She turned to see the Widow Mags, Bertha, and Evie all regarding her quizzically.

"Is something the matter?"

Caitlyn hesitated, then smiled and shook her head. "No, nothing. Just... my imagination, I think."

Nevertheless, she reached out and pulled the window shut, latching it firmly before stepping away.

CHAPTER FOUR

"Well, Evie and I had better head off," said Bertha, after they had cleaned up the kitchen, put away all the ingredients, and carefully stored the new batch of chocolate sauce. She started to pick up her wicker basket, then stopped and said, "Oh! I almost forgot—"

She reached into the basket and took out two tiny bouquets of herbs and flowers, bundled together and tied with twine. She handed one to Caitlyn and the other to her daughter.

"A Midsummer bouquet with a protective charm… Carry it with you and it will keep you from harm," she explained with a smile. "Midsummer is the traditional time for gathering magical and medicinal plants—many are most potent at this time of the year—and it is part of the ritual of celebrating the summer solstice."

Caitlyn held the bouquet to her nose. A sweet and spicy fragrance rose from the tiny bundle.

"Verbena, rosemary, fennel, dog rose, elder, and—most important of all—St. John's wort," said Bertha softly. "Ancient herbs with powerful magic that will protect you and keep you safe." Then she smiled and gave them a conspiratorial look. "And there is another old tradition as well: it is believed that if you place the bouquet under your pillow before you go to sleep on Midsummer's Eve, you will dream of the man you are going to marry."

Caitlyn saw Evie blush and felt her own cheeks warm slightly. It was embarrassing—she wasn't some thirteen-year-old schoolgirl having her first crush—and yet, she hoped fervently that Bertha couldn't read her thoughts nor see the image of the tall, handsome man that had flashed in her mind.

"Uh..." Caitlyn cleared her throat and gave a forced laugh. "They're quite quaint, aren't they, these traditions?"

"That's one of the less ridiculous ones," the Widow Mags growled. "There are some very silly customs going around, based on half-baked ideas about magic and witchcraft... Things like leaping through bonfires on Midsummer's Eve for good luck. Good luck, my broom! More likely to get a burnt bum," she said in disgust.

"Oh, don't forget the belief that if you wash your face with the dew of Midsummer's Day morning, the old will grow young and the young will grow more beautiful." Bertha laughed. "I've been trying that for several years now but, sadly, I think that one is a complete myth," she said, touching her wrinkles ruefully.

"But it *is* true, isn't it, that on Midsummer's Eve, the veil between the worlds is particularly thin?" Evie asked. "That it's easier to see magical beings, who can trespass between the realms?"

"That is true," the Widow Mags said, her voice becoming serious. "And you would do well to remember that. So many of the modern Midsummer celebrations are mindless acts of revelry. People have no respect or understanding of the ancient customs. But never forget, the old magic is still there, ready to be summoned at any time."

***

After Bertha and Evie left, Caitlyn helped the Widow Mags check that all the doors were locked and the lights turned off, then she headed tiredly to bed. But as she put her foot on the first step of the spiral staircase leading up to her attic bedroom, she hesitated. Turning back quickly, she called out:

"Grandma..." She faltered slightly. It was only a week ago that she had learnt that the old witch was her maternal grandmother and it still felt strange to call her by that name. She cleared her throat and tried again. "Grandma, I was wondering... how come the chocolate sauce doesn't make people fall in love?"

The Widow Mags paused in the doorway of her own bedroom. "What do you mean?" she asked.

"Well, if the love potion really works then… wouldn't adding it to the chocolate sauce make those who tasted the sauce fall in love with other people?"

"It isn't as simple as that," said the Widow Mags. "I would never use the love potion in its crude, concentrated form. I want a more subtle effect and for that, I combine it with *cacao*, which has an ancient magic of its own." She gave a cackling laugh. "People have been aware for a long time that chocolate makes you feel good. Human scientists use complicated words like 'endorphins'—but really, it is simply the magic held within the *cacao* bean, which is so potent that even just eating chocolate, without any spells, gives you feelings of bliss and happiness. I have simply enhanced that feeling by adding a little bit of the 'love-in-idleness' flower extract."

"So… you mean, when people taste the sauce, they feel like they're falling in love?"

"The same feelings of happiness and excitement, yes. It lifts their mood and makes them feel more positive about their lives. But it is fleeting and it does no harm. It is a little fun I have each year around the time of the summer solstice."

"What if someone does drink the concentrated

love potion? Would that make them fall in love?"

The old witch grew serious. "Love magic is a complicated thing. Certainly, a potion can be created to evoke the feelings of yearning and desire, of tenderness and contentment, but a spell is also required to direct those feelings towards the right person. And that can be tricky—very tricky. In fact, it is one of the most difficult forms of magic to master, and, in any case, it is not a skill that is encouraged."

"Why not?" asked Caitlyn, surprised.

"Because love magic is not something one should meddle with."

"But... but if it could help two people who could be happy together... and it's just because one of them is very shy and hasn't got much... um... confidence..." said Caitlyn, thinking of Evie's face when Chris Bottom had walked into the shop earlier that day. "I mean, it wouldn't really do any harm, would it? It would just be like having a bit of help—like using make-up to make yourself look prettier so that someone would notice you..."

The Widow Mags gave her a piercing look and Caitlyn squirmed. She suddenly realised that the old witch had misunderstood and was probably thinking that Caitlyn wanted the potion for herself!

"Using a love potion is very different to using a bit of mascara," the Widow Mags said at last. "It is not simply enhancing your best features—it is forcing others to bend to your will."

"But they might have fallen in love anyway—" Caitlyn protested.

"Yes, but of their own accord. Using magic to force others to surrender their emotions against their will is one of the most despicable forms of witchcraft," the Widow Mags said, her eyes flashing. "It is the kind of thing practised in the Dark Arts and what has led to so much fear and suffering through the ages. Yes, it can sometimes be used in the right way by a skilled and powerful witch... but never without consequences." Then her expression softened and she added, "Besides, even if it worked fine and there were no repercussions, it would never make you happy. You would always wonder if that love was real and deserved, and the doubt would fester inside you. Love, more than anything in the world, must be given freely."

The old witch's words echoed in Caitlyn's mind as she undressed and prepared for bed. A part of her still felt unconvinced. She couldn't help thinking that it would take so little to make Evie happy—a drop of potion, that was all—and what did it matter if there was a bit of "outside intervention"? She was sure that if Chris had something to help him see past Evie's awkward manner and (temporarily!) unfortunate appearance, he would find her endearing and attractive...

Caitlyn didn't realise that she had drifted off to sleep until she awoke, drenched in sweat and breathing quickly. She had been dreaming—it was a dream she'd had before, of fire blazing around her, the orange flames flickering like sinister tentacles and the heat pulsing in her face.

She sat up slowly, pushing the sheets away from her heated body, and trying to calm her breathing. Then she noticed something which made her heart start racing again. An orange glow was coming through the open bedroom window. She had seen that glow once before—on the first night she arrived in Tillyhenge, actually—and she scrambled out of bed now, rushing across the room to the window, wondering if she would see the same thing she had seen that night.

Yes. It was there: a bonfire at the top of the hill behind the cottage.

Caitlyn whirled and snatched up her old cardigan to cover her bare shoulders, then ran out of the room and down the spiral staircase as fast as she could. She charged through the kitchen and out into the garden. It registered briefly that the back door had been open but she barely paused to think about it—all she was focused on was getting to the top of the hill to see who had lit the bonfire.

But as she ran down the path and out of the cottage garden, she tripped over something and went crashing to the ground. She landed with a thump that knocked the breath from her and lay for a moment, panting and stunned. Then she groaned and rolled over, heaving herself to her knees.

What had she stumbled over? From the light of

the moon, which was now high in the sky, she saw a long dark shape huddled next to her. Putting her hands out tentatively, she groped around in the dark, then jerked back, her heart pounding.

It was a dead body.

CHAPTER FIVE

For a moment, Caitlyn thought that she was still caught in her dream—that the dead body lying next to her was simply a figment of her imagination. But as she stretched her hands out nervously once more and her fingers encountered clammy flesh, she realised that this was horrifyingly real.

Maybe they're not dead, she thought wildly. *Maybe they're just hurt or unconscious...*

But as she leaned down and strained her ears for the sound of breathing, her senses confirmed what her instinct had told her the minute she found the body. No one alive could be that still. *Who was it?* Her heart pounding uncomfortably, Caitlyn struggled to shift the body so that she could see the face better. The head lolled sideways and moonlight fell on the waxen features. Caitlyn felt a jerk of recognition.

It was Mandy Harper.

What was she doing here? Caitlyn stared blankly at the girl's body. There were no obvious signs of injury—no wounds or blood or evidence of any weapons; it was almost as if the girl had fallen backwards and dropped dead. Caitlyn shivered.

Then she noticed that the girl's right hand was flung outwards, her fingers curled tightly—almost as if she had been clutching something which had been torn from her grasp. Caitlyn narrowed her eyes. There was still something caught between the girl's fingers—a length of string, with a piece of yellowed paper attached. A label.

Frowning, Caitlyn leaned closer. There was a dark scrawl on the label—it was hard to make out the letters in the weak light of the moon—but she thought she saw the word "*Love*". She reached out, but before she could pull the label from the dead girl's fingers, she felt a hand clamp down suddenly on her shoulder.

Caitlyn screamed and jerked around. A thin, balding old man was stooped over her, peering down quizzically. He was wearing a shabby black suit, which looked like a relic from the last century, and he had two gaping holes in his mouth where his upper canine teeth ought to have been.

"Viktor!" cried Caitlyn, clutching a hand to her heart. "Don't sneak up on me like that!"

"Sneak? Vampires do not sneak," said the old

man indignantly. "We *glide* through the darkness."

"Yeah, right, blunder through the darkness would be more accurate," muttered Caitlyn, thinking of how blind Viktor was.

"Eh?"

"Nothing. Viktor, what are you doing here?"

"I was simply coming back to the cottage garden and saw you huddled there... Have you seen my fangs, by the way? I was sure I'd left them here on the wall, by the gooseberry bush. I had to take them out, you see, because the seeds kept getting stuck between the gaps in the teeth—*most* annoying—although I must say, the gooseberries were well worth the trouble. A bit tart, perhaps, but wonderful bursts of flavour—"

"Viktor," Caitlyn interrupted him, "have you been hanging around here all night?"

"Here?" The old man looked around the garden. "What would I hang on? You do realise that I am not a runty little vampire bat—we fruit bats can weigh over three pounds, you know, and we require good sturdy branches to suspend from."

"No, no, not hanging literally—I meant, have you been spending time here in the cottage garden? Did you see anyone loitering about a bit earlier? Maybe two people struggling?" Caitlyn looked at him hopefully.

Viktor shook his head. "I've been over at the Manor all afternoon—marvellously comfortable nook in the Library, you know, perfect for an afternoon kip. This is the first time I've returned."

Caitlyn sighed and turned back to the body. Viktor leaned over to look as well.

"Great garlic!" he cried, doing a double take. "She's dead."

"Yes, I'd sort of noticed that," said Caitlyn dryly. "We have to call the police."

She thought of her mobile phone in her room and wondered if she would be able to get a signal. She had got fairly used to the inexplicable "black hole" over Tillyhenge, which meant that phone reception and the internet were patchy and unreliable, and most of the time she didn't even miss it. But tonight, for once, she wished she had reliable telecommunication. "I'm going to have to use the landline in the chocolate shop—"

"Fear not, *I* can summon the police constables," said Viktor, puffing his bony old chest out importantly.

"No, you can't," Caitlyn protested.

"Why not?"

"Well, because you're..." She hesitated. Even after several weeks of getting used to the idea, she still found it strange to say it. "You're a vampire."

"And why should that prevent me from summoning the police? Vampires are law-abiding citizens too!" said Viktor huffily.

"Yes, but..." Caitlyn trailed off, not sure how to word it diplomatically. The police were either going to see a fuzzy brown fruit bat or a crazy old man with missing teeth. Neither was likely to be taken seriously.

"Ten minutes."

There was a murmur of wings and, when she turned to look again, the old vampire was gone. Caitlyn hesitated, wondering if she should ring the police herself anyway, then decided to give Viktor the benefit of the doubt. She'd wait ten minutes and see. In the meantime, she went to rouse the Widow Mags, who had surprisingly slept through all the commotion. Then something compelled her to go back outside again—maybe just to check if the body was really there or if she had imagined it all.

As she stood looking down at the dead girl, Caitlyn suddenly remembered the bonfire. In all the excitement, she had completely forgotten about the reason she had got out of bed in the first place. She looked up at the top of the hill. As she had expected, it was dark, with no sign of the eerie orange glow. She sighed. That mystery would have to remain unsolved again.

Then, as she dropped her gaze, she saw something glittering in the grass a few feet away from the body. Caitlyn walked over and picked it up, frowning as she examined the object. It was a pink, heart-shaped rhinestone, like the kind of fake jewel you might see decorating handbags and tiaras. She wondered if it had been torn off Mandy's clothing, but when she returned to the body, she couldn't see any sign of sequins or diamanté anywhere on the dead girl. Which meant that it was probably something the murderer had inadvertently dropped at the scene of the crime. Caitlyn held it up to the light again and turned it over. It was definitely a very feminine accessory, something a teenage girl might wear, perhaps...

The sound of engines in the lane at the front of the cottage, followed by car doors slamming and the sound of a police radio, interrupted her thoughts. To Viktor's credit, the police had arrived in record time. Caitlyn didn't know how he had managed it—she had visions of a fuzzy brown fruit bat flying into the nearest police station and squeaking bossily at a couple of bemused police officers—but she was too relieved to care.

Shoving the rhinestone into her cardigan pocket, she hurried back into the cottage to let the police in.

CHAPTER SIX

"And you say you didn't hear anything? You didn't wake up, even after the scream?" Inspector Walsh, the grizzled CID detective normally in charge of serious crime in the local area, eyed the Widow Mags sceptically from across the kitchen table.

"I already told you—I took a sleep tonic before bed," the old witch snapped. "I haven't been sleeping well—my arthritis has been particularly bad lately—and my daughter, Bertha, made up a tonic for me. It must have been stronger than I thought."

"Hmm..." The inspector looked down at his notes. "And how well did you know the dead girl?"

"Seen her about the village. She's at school with my granddaughter, Evie," the Widow Mags said.

"But I understand she came to *Bewitched by*

Chocolate earlier yesterday?"

"Yes, but I didn't see her. I was out most of the day gathering herbs in the forest. Caitlyn, here, was minding the shop for me."

Caitlyn sat up straighter and tried to stifle a yawn as the detective turned to her. It had been a long night so far. By the time the police had secured the crime scene, the Forensics team had arrived to do a sweep of the area, and the ambulance had taken the body away, it was the early hours of the morning. She had been relieved when Inspector Walsh finally sat them down for questioning. Now that the adrenaline from the initial shock of the discovery was fading away, she felt drained and exhausted, and just wanted to go to bed.

The only thing that made her feel slightly better was that the inspector looked quite dishevelled too, his hastily-donned shirt and trousers very different from his usual appearance of sombre suit and neatly-groomed moustache. Then her eyes slid to the man on his other side, who had also obviously dressed in a hurry and yet whose unkempt appearance did nothing to detract from his good looks. In fact, with his jaw unshaven and dark hair slightly mussed, Lord James Fitzroy—the owner of Huntingdon Manor and the surrounding estates—looked even more broodingly handsome than normal. Caitlyn winced as she thought of how she must look, with her tangled hair, face pale with fatigue, and dressed in a faded cotton sleep vest and shorts, covered only by her old cardigan. She sighed inwardly. Why did she always have to meet James Fitzroy looking her worst?

"And you, Miss Le Fey—did you know Mandy Harper?" asked Inspector Walsh.

Caitlyn snapped her attention back to him. "Yesterday was the first time I'd met her. She came to the shop late afternoon."

"Did she buy anything?"

Not if she could have got away with stealing it, Caitlyn thought. Aloud, she said, "Yes, some chocolate truffles."

"How did she seem when you saw her?"

Caitlyn hesitated. What should she say? *"Like a nasty, malicious bully and a shallow flirt"*? She cleared her throat and said, "She seemed fine. Very chatty and happy."

"And I understand she left in the company of a young man named Chris Bottom?"

"Yes, but surely you don't think—Chris wouldn't have anything to do with her death!"

"He was one of the last people to see her alive," said the inspector evenly. "But don't worry, he'll have a chance to give his account. We shall be questioning him later today."

"So… so you're treating this as murder then?" asked Caitlyn.

The inspector inclined his head. "Yes, we're treating it as a suspicious death."

"But how did she die? I didn't see any signs of

injury on her!"

He hesitated, as if debating whether to tell her, then said, "The forensic pathologist will need to do an autopsy to confirm, but he thinks it may have been a blow to the head."

"You mean someone hit her?"

"I would prefer not to speculate further at this point," said Inspector Walsh. He gave Caitlyn a sharp look. "Would anyone have reason to hit her? Did Mandy Harper have enemies? Someone who might have wanted to do her harm?"

Caitlyn swallowed, thinking uneasily of Evie's flushed face and her fingers clenched white around the mug handle, and hearing once again her cousin's shrill voice saying: *"I hate her! I HATE HER! ...I wish Mandy Harper would drop dead!"*

She shrugged. "Um... I wouldn't know. As I said, I only met her for the first time yesterday... but... but I think you're following the wrong angle," she added hastily. "I don't think Mandy was killed because of a grudge—I think she was killed because she had something that the murderer wanted." She looked at him earnestly. "There was a paper label in one of her hands, which was probably attached to a bottle. I think it was a bottle from the stillroom here in the cottage—I think somebody wanted that bottle and they took it from Mandy... Maybe there was a struggle and—although I don't know why Mandy had the bottle in the first place... I found the back door open, though, and I'm sure we locked it before going to bed, so someone must have broken in and—"

"Are you talking about this?"

Inspector Walsh put a clear plastic bag on the table between them. Sealed inside the bag was a yellowed paper label, still with the string attached. Caitlyn nodded and started to speak again but the inspector held his hand up to stop her and looked at the Widow Mags instead.

"Do you recognise this?"

"It looks like one of the tags I use to label my bottles and vials," said the Widow Mags, furrowing her brow. She pulled the bag towards her to get a better look and Caitlyn gave a little gasp as the words written on the label showed clearly now in the light of the kitchen.

"It's the love potion!" she cried.

"Love potion?" said Inspector Walsh, his brows drawing together. "What nonsense is this?"

"That label is from a vial of extract taken from the 'love-in-idleness' flower," said the Widow Mags calmly.

She got up from the table and went to the stillroom. Caitlyn could see that the cupboard inside was open. She knew from what the police had said earlier that it had been found in that state. It looked like Mandy—or someone else—had sneaked into the kitchen and been helping themselves to something from the stillroom.

The old witch returned to the table. "I just

checked—the vial is missing."

"Why would anyone want to steal this... this 'love-in-idleness' extract?" asked Inspector Walsh.

"It is a valuable ingredient with powerful properties."

"Such as making people fall in love?" asked the inspector sarcastically. "And I suppose you think someone murdered Mandy Harper to get their hands on this 'magic' potion?"

"There were two people in the shop yesterday who were certainly very interested in this potion," Caitlyn shot back. "Either of them could have wanted it badly enough to kill for it." Quickly, she told him about the eccentric Professor Ruskin.

"You expect me to believe that a respected academic would murder a girl just to get his hands on a fictional love potion?" demanded Inspector Walsh.

"But that's just the point!" said Caitlyn. "Getting hold of the love potion would prove that it's *not* fictional—it would be the culmination of his life's work! Professor Ruskin is obsessed with *A Midsummer Night's Dream*; he'll do anything to prove that Shakespeare's play was inspired by real life."

"Hmm..." Inspector Walsh sounded deeply sceptical. "And the other? You said there were two people."

"Oh... yes, a businessman called Dennis Kirby," said Caitlyn.

James Fitzroy spoke up for the first time. “I know Kirby,” he said with a grimace. “He owns a chocolate-making factory and supplies many of the cafés and supermarkets in the local area. His products are fairly low-quality, mass-market fare, high in sugar and artificial flavours. I’m sorry to say that I have never liked him much. When he first heard that we were opening up the Manor to the public and offering refreshments to the tourists, he tried to get a contract as a supplier and I found his manner extremely pushy, bordering on obnoxious.”

“What was Kirby doing here?” asked the inspector.

“He wanted me to sell him the recipe for my chocolate sauce,” growled the Widow Mags. She nodded at the label on the table. “Especially the secret ingredient in my recipe… which happens to be the ‘love-in-idleness’ extract.”

“So you think Kirby could have murdered the girl to get his hands on the vial?” The inspector sounded deeply sceptical again. “And how would he even know that this… er… love potion was used in your recipe?”

“He might have been eavesdropping at the kitchen window,” said Caitlyn suddenly. “Last night, when we were making up a new batch of the chocolate sauce, I heard a noise at the window. When I went over to look, I thought I saw a figure hurrying away.”

“Man or woman?”

Caitlyn shrugged. "I couldn't really tell. It was too dark. But it could easily have been Dennis Kirby. He'd left only a couple of hours earlier and he seemed determined to get the recipe, by any means. He could have sneaked back... and if he was listening at the window, then he might have also seen where the vial was kept, so he could have planned to come back for it after everyone had gone to sleep."

"But it's Mandy Harper who seems to have stolen the vial, not Dennis Kirby," the inspector reminded her. "The label was found in her fingers. How do you explain how *she* knew where the vial was kept and why *she* would want to steal it?"

Caitlyn hesitated. "Well, maybe it wasn't Dennis Kirby at the window then—maybe it was Mandy! And she stole it because... because she wanted to use the love potion to make someone fall in love with her and—"

The inspector made an impatient sound. "Are you now suggesting that Mandy Harper was after this love potion as well? Miss Le Fey, do you think the whole village of Tillyhenge is desperate for a magical aphrodisiac?"

Caitlyn flushed and looked down at the table. Even to herself, she had to admit that the whole thing sounded far-fetched and ridiculous. After all, if Mandy had been the one eavesdropping and not Dennis Kirby, then why would the businessman come to the cottage at all? Which would mean that it hadn't been him who had taken the vial off Mandy—which would mean that he wasn't the murderer. The same argument applied for Professor Ruskin. So who did murder the girl and take the potion?

"Who else knew where you kept this... er... love potion?" Inspector Walsh turned back to the Widow Mags.

"Only myself, Caitlyn, my daughter Bertha, and my granddaughter Evie," replied the old woman. "They watched me make the chocolate sauce last night and saw where I stored it."

"And the key to the cupboard door?"

Widow Mags hesitated. "That door is not locked by a key."

"You keep it unlocked?"

Caitlyn saw the old witch hesitate again, obviously wondering how to answer the inspector's question truthfully without admitting that the cupboard door had been locked by magic.

"It is secured in such a way that would be hard for random strangers to open," she said at last.

Caitlyn thought uneasily of Evie again. She had a vivid memory of the naked longing on her young cousin's face as the girl had watched the Widow Mags replace the love potion in the stillroom cupboard. And Evie certainly had the magical skills to open that door.

"Well, my men have dusted the cupboard for fresh prints so we shall see... In the meantime, I think that will be all my questions for now," said Inspector Walsh, rising from the table. "Unless you have anything to add, Miss Le Fey? As the person who was first on the scene, anything you might have noticed could be crucial in helping to find Mandy Harper's killer."

Caitlyn slid her hand into her cardigan pocket and felt the hard edges of the rhinestone dig into her fingers. She knew that she ought to tell the police about finding it near the body but something held her back.

"No, nothing," she said firmly.

"Right. In that case..." The inspector turned back to the Widow Mags. "My constable will take a copy of all the receipts from your transactions yesterday. We'd like to track down the customers who were here, especially the ones who might have been in the store at the same time that Mandy came in, and question them. One of them might have noticed something."

"Perhaps that could wait until morning?" James suggested politely. "I'm sure Caitlyn and the Widow Mags would be grateful for a few hours' sleep first, Inspector."

Caitlyn felt a rush of gratitude towards James and, in spite of the embarrassment over her dishevelled appearance, she was glad that he was there. There was something about his quiet authority and commanding presence that was very reassuring. And even though he had no official standing with the police, it was easy to see that Inspector Walsh respected him greatly, always including him in reports for any criminal investigation.

The inspector gave a grudging nod. "Yes, well, all right—I'll have my constable come back later in the morning."

"I'll see them out," Caitlyn told her grandmother, seeing her face drawn with tiredness.

The old woman nodded gratefully and disappeared into her bedroom. Caitlyn walked James and the policemen to the front door, but although the inspector and his constable walked quickly away down the lane, James lingered behind.

"Are you sure you're all right?" he asked, his grey eyes warm with concern.

"Yes, thanks... It was a bit of a shock finding the body but I'm fine now." Caitlyn looked at him shyly. "It's good of you to come out in the middle of the night. You're hardly going to get any sleep now."

"Not at all," said James. "I wanted to be there. I wouldn't want you facing police questioning on your own."

"Oh..." Caitlyn felt a rush of warmth at the thought of James Fitzroy feeling such tender concern for her. "I... I didn't realise that you'd come just for me."

"Well..." James smiled. "You know, the welfare of all the tenants in the village is my concern."

Caitlyn dropped her eyes. "Oh, yes, of course...

after all, Mandy is the daughter of one of your farmers... you'd want to be involved in the investigation to find her killer."

James cleared his throat. "Er, yes... that too."

They stood in silence for a moment and Caitlyn was suddenly aware of how alone they were, in the empty lane in front of the chocolate shop, with the darkened village around them and everyone still fast asleep. It felt almost like... *an illicit tryst.* She flushed and chided herself for her presumptuous imagination.

From somewhere in the darkness came the sound of a cockerel crowing in the distance—obviously overly-eager to announce the new day—and Caitlyn realised that the night was almost over. She'd be lucky to get to bed before dawn. And yet suddenly, she felt wide awake and very conscious of the tall man standing next to her. She stole a glance at him, just in time to catch him looking at her. He looked quickly away, then hesitated and turned back to her.

"Caitlyn... ever since you came to Tillyhenge, I—" He broke off and leaned slowly towards her.

Caitlyn stared up at him as he came closer... and closer... James reached out a hand towards her face and her breath caught in her throat. Her heart hammered wildly. She closed her eyes, expecting to feel his hand tenderly brush her cheek...

"You've got something in your hair."

Huh? Caitlyn's eyes snapped open and she found

James staring quizzically at her—or rather, at a point above her right ear. His hand, which had been hovering next to her face, lifted and plucked something out of her hair. She looked up and saw something round, hairy and green, and stifled a scream.

"What the—?" James started laughing. "It's all right... it's just a gooseberry."

"A... *gooseberry?*" Caitlyn took the thing from him and held it up to the moonlight. It was a small green fruit, a bit similar to a grape, except a lot rounder and a lot hairier, with light green veining visible through the translucent skin. "Oh. This must be from the garden at the back of the cottage. Viktor was talking about—I mean, I noticed a gooseberry bush near the back wall, when I found the body."

"Better check to make sure you haven't got any more twigs in your hair. They can have sharp spines," said James.

"Uh... yes, thanks."

"Well, I'd better leave now and let you get to bed." James gave her a smile. "Sleep well."

"Thank you."

Swallowing a sense of regret and disappointment, Caitlyn watched him walk away, his long strides taking him swiftly down the lane until he disappeared into the darkness.

CHAPTER SEVEN

Caitlyn stepped into the cool, spacious interior of *Herbal Enchantments* and paused for a moment, looking around in appreciation. Just like the first time she had stepped into the store, she felt a sense of calm settle over her. Perhaps it was the soothing fragrances wafting from the natural soy candles, the herbal tea sachets and hand-made goat's milk soaps stacked on the shelves, or the soft, earthy tones of the décor. Or maybe it was just the gentle, magical aura that her aunt, Bertha, cast over the place. She may not have inherited the Widow Mags's special skill with chocolate but Bertha had a wonderful talent all her own.

And she had been accepted by the villagers in a way that her mother never had. Part of this may simply have been due to Bertha's warm personality and gentle, motherly manner, which encouraged many villagers to come to her shop for herbal remedies, rather than visit the local pharmacy. *Funny how many people are willing to overlook Bertha's "witch" associations when they can benefit from her healing skills*, Caitlyn thought cynically.

Two of them were in the store now, standing at the counter with Bertha, talking loudly about hay fever.

"...that balm you gave me last week, Bertha—my, it's worked a treat, it has! So I told Joy, here, that she had to come and see you too."

The other woman moaned, "My nose just keeps running... and, oh, my eyes get so red and itchy and I... ah...ahh...AHH...*ATCHOO*!" She clutched her nose with one hand and groped hastily in her handbag for tissues with the other.

"Well, this mixture should see you right," said Bertha soothingly. "It has elderflower, eyebright, feverfew, goldenrod, plantain, and sage, which all help to relieve hay fever symptoms. Ginger tea is very good too. If it doesn't work, come back and I'll give you some of my butterbur oil extract, but as that can cause side-effects, I'd prefer to try that last."

"Oh, thank y—*ATCHOO*!"

Caitlyn turned away from the counter and drifted down to the other end of the store, where she had spied Evie arranging natural loofah sponges on one of the shelves.

"Hi Evie," she said quietly.

The other girl jumped and looked around nervously. "Oh... it's you, Caitlyn."

"Have you heard about Mandy?"

Evie nodded, her face pale. "The police came to speak to Mum first thing this morning and they questioned me too."

"What did you tell them?"

"What do you mean?" The girl gave her a frightened look. "I... I just told them what happened yesterday: that I saw Mandy in class and then, after school, she came to the chocolate shop. And that was the last time I saw her."

"Did they ask you where you were at midnight last night?"

"Yes, I told them I was in bed."

Caitlyn hesitated, then dug her hand in her cardigan pocket and pulled out the rhinestone, holding it out on her palm. "Is this yours?"

"No."

Caitlyn stared at Evie, wondering if she was telling the truth. "I found it next to Mandy's body," she added. "I think the murderer might have dropped it—"

"Well, it's not mine!" Evie said.

Caitlyn saw a flash of fear in her eyes and her heart sank. "Evie, listen... if you're... er... in any trouble, you can tell me..." she said gently.

"Why... why do you think I'd be in trouble?" Evie asked, her voice higher than normal.

"Well, you—"

"Evie? Have you done the loofah, dear? If you're finished, I need you to help me with the aloe vera lotions," came Bertha's voice from the other side of the store.

"I've got to go," Evie mumbled, hurrying past Caitlyn.

Caitlyn sighed and left the store, chewing her lip in frustration. She knew that Evie was lying—the girl couldn't have looked more guilty if she tried!—but she didn't know how to get her cousin to confide in her. The question was, what was Evie lying about? Could she really have been involved in Mandy Harper's murder?

Caitlyn recoiled from the thought. No. She couldn't believe it. Evie could never murder anyone. But then she thought uneasily of her cousin's expression at the chocolate shop the day before, the way her face had been blotchy with distress and rage after Mandy's teasing. Anyone would be forgiven for wanting to hurt Mandy after the way Evie was treated yesterday. But even if Evie had been tempted to exact some kind of revenge, Caitlyn was sure that she would only seek to humiliate Mandy, not physically harm her. Something like the way the Widow Mags had once hexed her tormentors with chocolate warts, perhaps—embarrassing but not really hurtful.

But... what if Evie hadn't done it on purpose? Sometimes you weren't always in control of magic.

Anger or other extreme emotions could make you inadvertently use your witch abilities to "punish" others. Caitlyn knew this herself—in fact, although the person had deserved it, she still felt slightly ashamed of what she had done.

Before she could ponder further, Caitlyn's thoughts were interrupted by the sight of a familiar figure coming out of a building farther down the street. It was Professor Ruskin. He paused and looked furtively around, then darted around the side of the building and disappeared.

Caitlyn realised that it was the back of the village pub and, on an impulse, she ran down the street until she had reached the same corner. The front of the pub and the original buildings faced the village green, but there was an extension which ran along the back of the building and stretched sideways to meet the forest. A rear service door led out of the extension—this was the door which Professor Ruskin had come out of—and as Caitlyn followed his footsteps and rounded the corner, she found herself stepping into a wild, overgrown area at the edge of the forest.

She caught sight of a movement through the trees—Professor Ruskin hurrying deeper into the forest—and without thinking, she plunged after him. There wasn't enough undergrowth and the trees weren't dense enough to completely conceal her; if he had looked back, he would have been sure to see her. Luckily, though, once they were in amongst the trees, the professor seemed to relax and stop looking over his shoulder. In fact, Caitlyn could hear him humming a tune happily to himself as he made his way through the undergrowth.

They were moving fairly fast, taking a slightly curving route, and Caitlyn realised after a while that they were circling around the village, through the forest, and heading for the hill at the back of the Widow Mags's cottage. In fact, she could soon feel the ground begin to slope upwards beneath her feet and knew that they were climbing through the forest that covered one side of the hill. The professor seemed to know exactly where he was going—he didn't pause or hesitate—and Caitlyn had to work to keep up.

The dappled light around them was brightening now as the trees thinned and sunlight pierced the forest canopy. The next moment, Caitlyn caught a glimpse of the open hill through the trees ahead, a gentle curve of green grass, a flash of grey boulders, a triangle of blue sky, and she realised that they were coming out by the crest of the hill, next to the Tillyhenge stone circle.

An ancient landmark of mysterious origins, the stone circle was the source of countless local myths and legends, and was the reason for much of Tillyhenge's fame as the "magical" village in the Cotswolds. The large sarsen boulders were laid out in a perfect circle atop the hill, and were supposed to be the misshapen forms of ancient warriors, frozen by magic but ready to awaken one day. They were also supposed to be uncountable and immovable, with any attempt to remove one leading to death and disaster, and the circle itself was believed to conceal a doorway to the Otherworld, sitting as it did on the intersection of several ley lines.

Of course, Caitlyn knew that most of these colourful tales were probably created or embellished for the tourists' benefit, but with what she had learnt since coming to Tillyhenge, she knew better now than to just dismiss local legends as "silly nonsense". After all, weren't "witches" supposed to only exist in folktales as well? And it was certainly true that she had been unable to count the stones, no matter how many times she had tried.

She paused at the edge of the forest, half-concealed behind a large beech tree, and watched in bemusement as Professor Ruskin ran out onto the open hilltop, waving his arms, and cavorted around the outside of the stone circle. *Poor thing—he really* has *lost all his marbles*, she thought. Then he stopped all of a sudden and crouched down beside one of the boulders. Caitlyn craned her neck to see what he was doing but his back blocked her view of his hands. Was he looking at something on the ground?

Curiosity got the better of her and she left the shelter of the trees, moving furtively closer. He was so absorbed that she thought she could get close enough to take a peek, then retreat again without him noticing. Then her right foot sank into the ground, making her cry out in surprise: she had stepped into a rabbit hole concealed beneath a tuft of grass. Annoyed with herself, she quickly pulled her foot out. But it was too late.

When she looked up, she found herself staring straight into Professor Ruskin's surprised brown eyes.

CHAPTER EIGHT

Caitlyn opened her mouth, trying to think of a good excuse for why she was up here at the top of the hill, but before she could speak, the professor beamed at her and beckoned her towards him urgently.

"My dear! Would you look at this! I can hardly believe my luck!"

Caitlyn joined him and looked down at what he was pointing at. It was an ugly red mushroom, covered in little white warts, growing in the shade of the stone boulder.

"Er... um... is that a rare species of fungus or something?"

"No, no, my dear, it is a well-known toadstool—*Amanita muscaria*—the Fly Agaric mushroom. Commonly found in woodlands... and often growing in fairy rings!" he said, his eyes glowing with excitement. "And now I find it here, growing around the stone circle... isn't that just wonderful?"

"Er..."

"Don't you see? It's proof!"

"Proof?"

"Yes, further proof that this forest is the enchanted forest in *A Midsummer Night's Dream.* When I saw the stone circle, I just knew that it was the spot where King Oberon and Queen Titania danced with their fairy folk! After all, you would expect the king and queen of fairies to grace a much more impressive structure than a normal mushroom circle found in the forest. And now, I have definitive evidence!" He gestured to the toadstool at their feet.

Caitlyn didn't see how finding an ugly red mushroom was evidence of anything but she kept her thoughts to herself. Instead, she started to step through the gap between the two nearest boulders and walk into the stone circle. But she had barely taken a step when the professor grabbed her arm and yanked her back.

"What are you doing?" he gasped.

"What do you mean?" said Caitlyn, trying to wrench her arm out of his grasp. He was much stronger than he looked; his frail-looking hand was clamped around her arm like a vice.

Professor Ruskin put his face very close to hers and hissed angrily, "Don't you know anything, girl?

One must never enter a fairy ring unprotected! It's extremely dangerous—you could lose your mortal soul to the fairy folk!"

"Oh, that's a bit ridiculous, don't you think?" said Caitlyn impatiently. "Loads of tourists come here every day and—"

She broke off as the professor suddenly grabbed her wrist and began to run around the stone circle.

"Wait… what are you doing?" cried Caitlyn, stumbling as she was pulled along.

"Must–run–around–the–circle–nine–times…" Professor Ruskin panted. "Deosil, mind, not widdershins…"

"Widder–what?" said Caitlyn, struggling to keep up. For an old man, he could sure run fast!

"Widdershins!" he gasped. "Widdershins… in an anticlockwise direction… keep to the left… very unlucky…" He puffed. "If you walk widdershins around a fairy circle, the fairies will hold you in thrall—you will be in their power! But if you go around in the opposite direction—deosil—that will break the fairy magic—"

"Professor… I don't… this is crazy…" They had completed four circles now and Caitlyn was starting to feel a stitch in her side. "Professor! We've got to stop—"

"No!" His hand clamped around her wrist even harder as he put on another burst of speed. "Once one starts, one cannot stop!"

Finally, staggering and gasping for a breath, they

completed the nine circles and stopped where they had started. Caitlyn collapsed against the boulder with the mushroom and leaned against it, trying to get her breath back. Resentfully, she rubbed her wrist, where bruises were beginning to show, and wished that she had never followed Professor Ruskin into the forest. He was standing next to her now, still rambling on about the fairy folk, and she wondered if she could creep away without him noticing. Then she heard him say something which made her freeze on the spot.

"...one must remember that at this time of the year, fairy magic is at its most powerful and most dangerous... Look at the poor girl who was murdered last night—maybe she would not have perished if she had not tried to steal a potion sacred to the fairies. But everyone knows that the 'love-in-idleness' flower should only be administered by Puck under King Oberon's orders and—"

"Wait, Professor—what did you say?" Caitlyn caught his arm.

He blinked at her owlishly though his spectacles. "I was merely commenting on the distressing news I heard this morning. I'm staying at the pub, you see, and Traci the barmaid told me about the murder."

"Yes, but how did you know that the stolen potion contained the extract of the 'love-in-idleness' flower?" Caitlyn frowned. The murder had occurred in the middle of the night; the police hadn't even finished taking statements until the early hours of this morning, and in any case, given Inspector Walsh's scepticism and scorn of anything to do with "magic", she was sure he wouldn't release details like that to the press.

"Oh." The professor gave her a guilty look, like a schoolboy caught out doing something naughty. "Well... er... that businessman told me."

"Which businessman?"

"That Kirby fellow... what's his name? David? Derek?"

"Dennis—Dennis Kirby."

"Yes, that's right. Dennis. He was staying the night at the pub as well and we had a drink together, just before bed. Well, quite a few drinks, actually." He gave a dry chuckle. "He became quite talkative and he was rather excited—claimed to have found a secret ingredient that was going to make him rich."

"And he told you that the secret ingredient was the 'love-in-idleness' flower extract?"

"Yes, but I had deduced it already!" Ruskin said proudly. "You see, when I heard you and that other young lady discussing your 'love potion', I already had my suspicions. And then Dennis let slip that the 'secret ingredient' he was pursuing was concocted from the juice of a flower that only blooms just before Midsummer's Eve. Well, naturally, one immediately thinks of Act 2, Scene 1 in *A Midsummer Night's Dream*!"

"Er... one does?"

He nodded eagerly. "Shakespeare talks of a flower with magical properties to make one fall in love…" He quoted:

"Yet marked I where the bolt of Cupid fell.
It fell upon a little western flower,
Before milk-white, now purple with love's wound.
And maidens call it love-in-idleness.
Fetch me that flower. The herb I showed thee once.
The juice of it on sleeping eyelids laid
Will make or man or woman madly dote
Upon the next live creature that it sees."

The old professor looked at Caitlyn triumphantly. "You see, my dear? I just knew it when I heard Kirby speak of it. It is the very same love potion that Puck administers to the lovers in the play! And when I challenged Kirby, he admitted that it was indeed called the 'love-in-idleness'." He clutched Caitlyn's arm, making her wince again. "If only I could have seen the potion myself… ohhh, it would have been the discovery of a lifetime! When you consider the scholarship value, the academic importance…" His voice was quavering with excitement and his eyes had taken on a manic gleam. "I would have papers published in all the top literary journals… maybe even a lead article in *Shakespeare Quarterly*… maybe a book deal… and I'd show all those idiots who'd laughed at me—"

"So Dennis Kirby said he knew where the love potion was kept?" asked Caitlyn, thinking that here was proof that the businessman was the eavesdropper at the window. Kirby couldn't have known that the potion was made from the "love-in-idleness" flower and that the flowers could only be harvested once a year, during the summer solstice, unless he had been listening when the Widow Mags was talking in the kitchen last night.

"He didn't actually say," said Professor Ruskin. "He merely talked of what he would do when he got hold of the potion..." Then he deflated, as if suddenly remembering something, and added mournfully, "But the potion has been stolen now, hasn't it? The young girl who was killed had been holding the love potion in her hands and it had been snatched from her."

"How did you know that?" demanded Caitlyn.

"The barmaid, Traci, told me. She heard it from Mrs Parsons, who had got it from Mrs Tripp, who spoke to one of the Forensics team when they went in to get some cigarettes from the post office shop..."

Caitlyn marvelled at the village grapevine. She wouldn't have been surprised if the local gossips knew more about the murder than the police did, by the end of the day. And knowing the way their minds worked, she was sure they would be pointing the finger at the two strangers staying in the village.

The question was—were they right to be

suspicious? Dennis Kirby certainly sounded like a prime suspect, but Caitlyn couldn't help thinking of the obsessive gleam in Professor Ruskin's eyes when he had been talking of the potion just now. He might've claimed that Kirby never told him where the potion was kept—but he could have been lying. And if he had known, would he have been able to resist the temptation of seizing the potion, which could represent the greatest achievement of his academic career? And if someone—such as Mandy Harper—had got in his way, could he have turned violent?

She narrowed her eyes and watched the old professor, who had finally decided that it was safe enough to step into the stone circle. He was now going around, pausing in front of each of the rocks and saying: "Hello! And how are you?"

Caitlyn shook her head in disbelief and turned away, starting to walk back down the hill. Honestly, could someone so batty plan a murder?

CHAPTER NINE

The village of Tillyhenge was roughly circular, with the village green filling the top portion of the circle and the pub at the very top edge, say at the twelve o'clock position—whilst *Bewitched by Chocolate*, the Widow Mags's chocolate shop, sat at the bottom end of the circle, at the six o'clock position, backed by the hill. The outside of the circle was surrounded on the left side by woodland forest and on the right side by open fields. To get from the pub and the village green to the chocolate shop—or vice versa—you had the choice of three routes: weaving through the village itself, going around the outside of the village through the forest, or going around the outside of the village on the other side, through the fields.

Caitlyn had come through the forest while

following Professor Ruskin, but now as she walked back down the hill, she decided to return to the village green using the other route. It was one she used less often—for some reason, taking the path through the forest always seemed quicker—but today, with the summer sunshine warm on her face, she decided it would be nicer to walk out in the open. As she began the curving route around the back of the houses, with the village to her left and the open fields on her right, she heard the sleepy lowing of cows. Soon a small herd came into sight. They were huddled together by the fence, munching on a patch of clover. They raised their heads and looked at her as she passed, flicking their ears and chewing slowly from side to side. Caitlyn found herself smiling. There was something so sweet about cows with their big, gentle eyes and placid expressions.

A little farther on, she noticed that a larger animal was standing alone in the other corner of the field. In fact, as she got closer, she realised that it was an enormous bull. He looked up eagerly as she approached and trotted to the fence, putting his head over and blowing gustily.

"Hello there," said Caitlyn with a smile.

He gave a loud *"MOOOO"* and stretched his thick neck towards her. He had huge limpid black eyes with ridiculously long eyelashes and a pale pink, velvety muzzle.

Caitlyn hesitated. All the general advice was to

avoid going near bulls. But this one looked so sweet and gentle, and was eyeing her with such wistful longing, that she found herself moving towards him before she realised what she was doing. Holding her hand out so that he could sniff her first, she took a step closer to the fence. He thrust his nose eagerly into her hand and she laughed as his whiskers tickled her palm.

Feeling braver, Caitlyn took another few steps until she was right beside the fence, reaching up tentatively to stroke his forehead. To her surprise, the bull suddenly turned his huge head and laid it on her shoulder. The weight of his head nearly bowled her over. She was reminded suddenly of James Fitzroy's English mastiff, Bran, who also liked to lean on those he loved.

Caitlyn laughed. "You're a bit of a smoocher, aren't you?"

He gave a loud *"MOOO"* in reply and swished his tail happily.

Carefully, she reached up and patted him on the side of his neck, then—feeling bolder—scratched him behind his ears. The bull closed his eyes in ecstasy, nuzzling closer to her.

"I see you've been getting acquainted with Ferdinand," came a voice from the field.

Caitlyn started and looked up. Beyond the bull's rump, she could see a middle-aged man coming towards her. From his outfit— green overalls tucked into black rubber boots—she guessed that he must be the farmer. He had a tanned, weather-beaten face that was good-looking in a rugged sort of way, and short, greying blond hair. He smiled as he approached her and something about his face seemed so familiar that Caitlyn felt as if she must have met him before. And yet she was sure this was the first time they'd met.

"Hi... sorry, I hope I wasn't doing anything I shouldn't," she said, gesturing apologetically to the bull who was still standing with his head on her shoulder.

The farmer chuckled. "Oh no, you couldn't be doing anything that would make Ferdinand happier. Loves his pats and rubs, he does."

"He's very gentle, isn't he?"

"He's a great big softie. His mother abandoned him when he was born and a friend o' mine hand-raised him. I reckon he thinks he's a big dog half the time. Follows you everywhere if you let him—even wants to come in the farmhouse!" he guffawed. Then he sobered. "To be honest with you, I think he's having a bit o' a hard time adjusting. Used to having company, you see, and he's been feeling lonely, out in the field by himself."

"Lonely? But what about—" Caitlyn gestured to the herd of cows on the other side of the field."

"Ah..." The farmer's face darkened. "Well, that's the problem. I got Ferdinand from my friend to keep as a stud bull. I have a small organic dairy farm, you see, and I wanted a bull to join the herd but..."

He shook his head in vexation. "The ladies won't have anything to do with him!"

"Oh." Caitlyn looked across at the herd again.

Next to her, the bull raised his head off her shoulder and also looked at them. He gave a tentative "*MOO…?*" and flicked his ears forward. The cows raised their heads and gave him an appraising stare, chewing thoughtfully, then they tossed their heads and turned in unison, presenting their bony backsides to him. Ferdinand's ears drooped and he lowered his head, blowing sadly.

"You see?" said the farmer. "Don't know what the problem is. It's not as if he isn't a big, strapping, handsome lad... and he's a real gentleman in the field too." He gave an exasperated laugh. "Maybe that's the problem. Not macho enough for 'em."

Caitlyn reached up to rub the silky ears again. The bull turned towards her and pressed his head to her chest, for all the world as if asking for a hug. Caitlyn patted his neck, feeling sorry for him.

"Have you asked the vet?"

The farmer nodded. "James sent for him immediately. Wonderful chap, the new Lord Fitzroy. Really been trying to help me figure things out. The vet came and checked Ferdinand over—and the girls too. We're just waiting for some tests now but he says they're all healthy." He shrugged. "'Course, the vet says I should just do what most dairy farmers do nowadays: use artificial insemination. But I like to let nature take its course, if I can.

That's why I got into the organic farming side o' things." He gave Ferdinand's rump a hearty slap and stepped back. "Anyway, I'd best be getting on. Nice to meet you, miss."

"You too." Caitlyn smiled at him. It was so refreshing to meet a villager who didn't treat her with suspicion or wariness. "Um... would it be okay if I came to see Ferdinand now and then... maybe bring him some treats?"

He grinned. "You feeling sorry for the big baby?"

"A bit," Caitlyn admitted, rubbing the bull's soft fur. "He does seem so lonely."

"Well, I'm sure he'd love a bit o' company and affection. And a treat or two wouldn't go amiss."

"What sorts of things do cows like? Are they like horses? Can you give them carrots and apples?"

"Sure, Ferdinand loves a bit o' apple. Beets too. And he likes the head o' broccoli and a bit o' cabbage now and then. Not too much, mind."

"I'll only give him a bit," Caitlyn promised. She smiled. "I'll be Ferdinand's girlfriend until he gets a better one."

The farmer roared with laughter. "You're a nice girl, miss."

"Please, call me Caitlyn."

He inclined his head, holding out a calloused hand. "Jeremy Bottom."

"Oh!" Caitlyn stared at him, suddenly realising why he felt so familiar. "You're Chris's father."

He smiled. "So you've met my lad."

"Just yesterday, actually. He came into the chocolate shop to pick up some chocolates for the Manor."

His face darkened. "Aye, the police were over at our place this morning, wanting to question Chris about Mandy Harper, seeing as he was the last person with her yesterday before she went home."

"Oh no, the police don't suspect Chris—"

"Reckon they would have, but luckily Mandy's parents confirmed that she was with 'em all evening until she went to bed at eleven. 'Course, the police were trying to suggest that there might have been something romantic-like between my Chris and Mandy. Kept asking him if he had gone out later to meet her." Jeremy made an impatient noise. "I soon put 'em right. Told 'em that Chris was home with me all evening and my boy isn't the type to go sneaking out at night to meet girls! They can ask my sister, Vera, too. She lives with us." He gave an emphatic nod.

"I'm sure James—Lord Fitzroy—would vouch for Chris as well," said Caitlyn. "I'm sorry Chris got mixed up in things. I guess it was one of those cases of being in the wrong place at the wrong time. If he hadn't come into the chocolate shop to pick up the samples for the Manor, he probably wouldn't even have met Mandy after school yesterday."

"Ah well, now... it's no matter. I suppose it's only right that the police should be doing everything to find the killer o' that poor girl." He gave her a curious look. "Now, you're the Widow Mags's long-lost granddaughter who's come over from America, that right?"

Caitlyn stared at him in surprise. She hadn't made a public announcement about her new-found relationship to Bertha and the Widow Mags, and she didn't think anyone knew about it yet. She should have known better. If the details of a murder enquiry could make its way around the village grapevine in less than half a day, the details of her mysterious heritage would surely have spread through all of Tillyhenge by now.

"Yes, that's right. I came over to England to find my family—my real family..." Caitlyn laughed. "It's funny, when I took lodgings at the chocolate shop, the last thing I expected was to discover that the Widow Mags was my grandmother!"

He gave an approving nod. "I reckon you'll be just what she needs—help bring her out o' herself a bit. She's a good woman, the Widow Mags, though a mite prickly, if you know what I mean... but her heart's in the right place." He chuckled as he saw Caitlyn's expression. "Yes, I know most o' the village is against her. There's all that talk about her being a witch... my sister Vera's one o' those always gossiping." He gave a shrug and smiled. "As I'm always saying to Vera—if there's going to be a witch in Tillyhenge, I am glad it's the Widow Mags."

CHAPTER TEN

When Caitlyn returned to the village green, she found a surprise waiting for her: a gleaming red sports convertible parked by the oak tree, its back seat piled high with monogrammed luggage. A curvaceous blonde girl wearing a hot pink Lycra mini-dress and designer shades was standing next to the car, chatting with Evie.

"Hi, Pomona!" Caitlyn called, hurrying towards the two girls, her face breaking into a smile. She had missed her American cousin and felt a thrill of pleasure at seeing her again.

"Caitlyn!" the blonde girl squealed and rushed forwards, throwing her arms around Caitlyn's neck and enveloping her in a crushing hug.

Caitlyn laughed and extricated herself from Pomona's embrace. You would have thought that they hadn't seen each other for decades and not just a week!

Pomona stepped back and beamed at Caitlyn, talking at top speed. "So did you miss me? What have you been doing? Learnt any new spells? Omigod, Caitlyn, I saw this thing on TV the other day—it was an old episode of *Buffy* where they, like, conjured up a rabbit—and I thought, it would be *so* cool if you could do it too! But maybe a chocolate rabbit… you know, like, chocolate Easter bunnies… and you could do them in different flavours… Or even other animals… A chocolate kitty would be cute—Oh, speaking of kitties, how's Nibs? Is he a lot bigger? I saw this gorgeous cat collar in Selfridges and I was like, I'm gonna get it for him—but it was in hot pink so then I thought maybe that was dumb for a boy… But you know, hot pink is all the rage at the moment… Omigod, what are you wearing? It's hideous! Caitlyn, you've gotta throw those jeans out. Imagine if James sees you… Hey, have you guys been out on a date? Have you kissed him yet—?"

"Pomona!" Caitlyn gasped, blushing. She caught sight of Evie standing to the side, grinning.

"What? You haven't kissed him yet?" Pomona groaned in frustration. "Caitlyn! What are you doing? Seriously, I set it all up perfectly for you! You guys should be making out in the back seat by now. Well, okay, maybe not the back seat. James is too much of the English gentleman. Maybe on, like, a beautiful antique *chaise longue*, then," said Pomona dreamily. "In that gorgeous romantic Victorian conservatory of his, up at the Manor—"

"Don't be ridiculous!" said Caitlyn, blushing even more. "There's nothing between James—I mean, Lord Fitzroy and me. He... he doesn't look at me that way at all."

"Yeah, and I wonder why," said Pomona darkly, eyeing Caitlyn up and down again. She let out another sigh of exasperation. "You're hopeless, Caitlyn! I can see I'm gonna have to get involved myself and—"

"Don't get any funny ideas," said Caitlyn quickly. The last thing she needed was to be dragged into Pomona's match-making schemes. Knowing her cousin, there was no telling what she might do. Pomona had no shame and firmly believed that the ends justified *any* means.

Sometimes Caitlyn wondered how they had ended up being best friends—they were so unalike. Pomona was glamorous, bubbly, and flamboyant, a classic Californian beauty with tanned brown limbs, big blue eyes, and wavy blonde hair styled in the latest fashion. Caitlyn, on the other hand, was as untrendy as you could get, shunning the limelight and preferring to spend the evening curled up with a good book rather than out at a party. She was shy about her looks and never knew how to make the most of her vivid red hair, milky complexion and hazel eyes.

And yet somehow their differences seemed to have brought them closer. Growing up, Caitlyn had always looked forward to the school vacations when her cousin would come to visit and join Barbara Le Fey's entourage for some time on the road. Caitlyn had no real friends of her own—her nomadic lifestyle and home-schooling made it difficult to meet local kids—and Pomona was like the sister she had never had. In fact, even after Barbara's Le Fey's recent death and the shock of discovering that she was adopted—that she and Pomona were not "cousins" by blood—the bond between them had never wavered.

When Caitlyn decided to come to England to search for answers about her past, Pomona had eagerly tagged along. And unlike Caitlyn, Pomona had always embraced the idea of witchcraft and magic, so she had been *delighted* when she discovered that they were real. She had also persuaded the Widow Mags to give the chocolate shop a much-needed makeover, scandalised the whole village with her outfits, started a viral social media campaign, and got herself kidnapped by a cold-blooded murderer—and that was just in her first two days in Tillyhenge!

Life might be a lot quieter when Pomona isn't around but it's a lot more boring too, Caitlyn thought with a smile. She was glad her cousin was back in the village.

"I didn't think you'd be back so quickly," she

said. "I thought you'd want to stay in London, with all the shopping and parties."

"Oh, the parties get a bit boring after a while," said Pomona with a shrug. Then she gave Caitlyn a coy smile. "Except one. That Sven Jordbro premier after-party—*that* was pretty awesome. And guess what?" She lowered her voice and spoke in a husky tone. "I met Thane Blackmort."

"The Black Tycoon?" Evie spoke up excitedly. "He's been in all the magazines and local papers recently! He's such a mystery, isn't he? Like, Mum says nobody knows where he came from or how he's made his money... What's he like?"

"So *hot*!" said Pomona, fanning herself dramatically. "Omigod, those piercing blue eyes of his—I swear, they're not human—and his sexy lips and that muscular butt—"

"You've seen his butt?" Caitlyn spluttered.

"No," said Pomona, giggling. "But I've seen the way he fills out a pair of pants and I can imagine what his naked butt looks like. Trust me, I've spent a *lot* of time imagining it, from every angle..." She waggled her eyebrows, grinning lasciviously. Then she turned to Evie. "Do any of the magazines have a picture of Blackmort's butt?"

"No," said Evie. "The tabloid ones are mostly of him taken at a distance. His bodyguards don't let anyone get too close to him. And the local papers... well, they're too angry to be interested in his bum."

"Angry?" said Caitlyn in surprise. "What are they

angry about?"

"His company, Blackmort Enterprises, has been buying up a lot of land in the local area and building modern developments. A lot of people think he's destroying the countryside. Mum says she's even heard rumours that Blackmort wants to buy a section of the Huntingdon Manor estates from Lord Fitzroy—the section with the hill and the forest and the stone circle. And he—" She broke off suddenly, her gaze going to something behind Caitlyn and Pomona.

Caitlyn whirled around as a *clop-clop-clop* sound reached their ears. A horse and rider were just emerging from one of the side lanes and stepping out onto the village green. An enormous grey stallion, with a dark-haired man astride him, handling the reins with practised ease, and a huge English mastiff lumbering in their wake.

Caitlyn's heart gave a jolt as it did every time she saw Lord James Fitzroy. He cut a particularly dashing figure today, in his breeches and black riding boots, and his unruly dark hair slightly wind-swept—like a hero straight out of the pages of Regency romance novel. A few tourists who were milling around looked up in admiration and whipped out their cameras as horse and rider trotted past them.

The stallion snorted and tossed its head, the powerful muscles bunching underneath his glossy grey coat, as James brought him to a stop next to them. Caitlyn watched nervously, suddenly tongue-tied, as James swung himself lightly off the horse and came forwards to meet them.

"Pomona! Great to see you back," he said, a welcoming smile on his handsome face. "It's a good thing I decided to ride Arion rather than drive, otherwise we wouldn't have come this way and we would have missed you."

The mastiff lumbered forwards happily, his wrinkled face pulled back in a wide doggie smile and his huge pink tongue hanging out. He shoved his nose into Pomona's crotch, lifting her feet clear off the ground as she squealed in surprise and flailed her arms around to keep her balance.

"Bran! Stop that!" cried James, all his aplomb instantly deserting him. "Stop that, you great oaf!"

He grabbed the huge dog by the collar and tried to pull him back. The mastiff stopped, confused, then tried to turn around, with Pomona still stuck astride his head. She yelped and flailed her arms even more wildly, then managed to swing one leg over the mastiff's back and slide off his neck, hopping sideways on one foot as she tried to regain her balance.

"Sorry," said James, looking flustered as he attempted to get his giant dog to sit. "He's... er... very well trained, really."

Bran sat down on his master's foot and James winced, then gave a rueful smile as all three girls laughed. Caitlyn was glad, though. Somehow, seeing James struggle with his big goof of a dog had made him seem more human and less like a fantasy romantic hero. She felt her nerves ease slightly.

"Hey, James—great to see you," drawled Pomona, throwing an arm around him and kissing him on the cheek with a casual ease that Caitlyn envied. "Did you miss me?" she asked, grinning at him.

James chuckled. "Oh, definitely. Huntingdon Manor has been very quiet without its lovely American guest. I hope you'll do us the honour of staying with us again."

Pomona clutched her heart theatrically. "Omigod—say that again, James!"

"Say what again?" He looked bewildered.

"The bit about me doing you an honour..." She giggled. "Man, I don't know anyone else who talks like they came out of the last century and gets away with it. Although anything sounds good with your sexy British accent."

James looked confused for a moment, then he laughed and said, "Okay, do you want to... er... crash at my digs?"

Pomona grinned at him again. "Oh no, the first version was way better!" Then she gestured to Evie and added, "Evie's invited me to stay with her and her mom, but thanks for the offer."

"In that case, perhaps you'd like to come to dinner at the Manor tonight?" James included Caitlyn and Evie in his smile. "All of you, of course—and Bertha and the Widow Mags too."

"Oh, thanks," said Evie, looking slightly over-awed. "Um… I'll have to check with Mum."

James looked at Caitlyn, who stammered, "Er… well, I…"

"Yeah, Caitlyn and I are definitely coming," Pomona said quickly. "What time?"

"Shall we say eight-thirty? I've given the police the use of the Library as an Incident Room for this murder investigation, you see, and they may be conducting interviews until quite late. I'd like to check in with Inspector Walsh before they leave for the day."

"Murder investigation?" Pomona turned wide eyes on Caitlyn. "Has there been another murder in Tillyhenge?"

Caitlyn noticed that Evie had stiffened at the mention of the murder and gone slightly pale.

She nodded to Pomona and said quietly, "One of the girls who lives in the village was killed last night. I found her body outside the back of the Widow Mags's cottage." She repressed a shudder at the memory.

"How was she killed?" asked Pomona.

"I…I've got to go," mumbled Evie suddenly. "I… um… Mum said she might need more goat's milk… for the soap…" Making vague gestures, she turned and hurried away.

Caitlyn watched her go with troubled eyes, whilst James answered Pomona's question.

"…so until the police get the autopsy report, we can't be sure, but Inspector Walsh is fairly certain that it was a blow to the head. The pathologist is doing the post mortem as a matter of urgency, so we should hopefully have the report by this evening. In the meantime, Inspector Walsh has told everyone in the village that they can't leave without informing the police."

Caitlyn swung around to face him, her previous shyness forgotten. "Including the two visitors? Professor Ruskin and Dennis Kirby?"

"Yes, especially them, in fact. They have to stay in the village until the police are done with their enquiries. Kirby kicked up quite a fuss—apparently he had been planning to return to Cheltenham this morning—but Inspector Walsh was adamant."

Caitlyn was glad to hear that the inspector was taking her suggestion seriously and treating the two men as suspects, even if he had been sceptical about the love potion.

"Has he questioned them?" she asked.

"I'm not sure, but if not, I'm sure he intends to soon. First, though, he wants to speak to the girl's family and close friends—those who may have seen her yesterday and who may know more about her recent movements and state of mind."

Caitlyn compressed her lips in annoyance and James noticed.

He said, "To be fair, there is no obvious connection between Mandy Harper and the two men. In fact, there is no evidence that she had any contact with either of them. In any murder enquiry, it would be normal to start the investigation with those who had direct interaction with the victim. And it is an accepted fact that most murder victims are killed by people familiar to them."

Caitlyn sighed impatiently, but she knew that James was right. And she couldn't really fault the police either. To a pragmatic man like Inspector Walsh, the fact that Mandy Harper had never spoken to or interacted in any way with either Professor Ruskin or Dennis Kirby meant a lot. The only tenuous connection was a love potion which Mandy had supposedly been holding when she was killed—and which the two men were supposedly interested in, based on its magical powers. Caitlyn sighed again. Even she had to admit that the whole thing sounded far-fetched and ridiculous when put like that.

James glanced at Arion, who was standing with his head down, relaxed, nearby. "Well, I'll look forward to seeing you later. I'd better get on now—Jeremy Bottom is expecting me."

"Oh, I just saw him," said Caitlyn. "Out in the field, with Ferdinand and the rest of the herd. We had a long chat."

"Ah, so he's told you about Ferdinand's dating problems?" said James with a smile.

"Dating problems?" Pomona's ears perked up.

Caitlyn laughed. "Nothing you can help with,

Pomona—not unless you've got some expertise in the bovine romance department. Ferdinand is a really sweet bull but the cows are snubbing him."

"A bull who has trouble with the ladies?" Pomona burst out laughing. "You're kidding!"

"No, it's been a big headache for Jeremy," said James. "He had such high hopes for Ferdinand as a stud bull and I think he's getting quite disheartened. He's a great farmer—he treats his cows really well. Especially with the state of modern dairy farming, it's fantastic that he's so committed to a completely natural, organic farming process and I really want to see him succeed."

"Maybe Ferdinand just needs a bit more time?" Caitlyn suggested.

"It's been nearly a month... and the cows don't seem to be any more taken with him." James gave a helpless shrug. "Anyway, I haven't spoken to Jeremy for a few days so I was planning to look in on him and see how things were."

He made as if to turn away, then paused and asked, "Did you manage to get some sleep after I left?"

"Ooh!" Pomona's ears really perked up this time. She eyed the two of them avidly. Caitlyn could see her adding up two and two and making five, and realised that her cousin had completely misinterpreted James's question.

She said hurriedly, "It's not what you think—"

"You big fat liar!" cried Pomona, laughing.

"Telling me there's nothing between you and James when you guys are, like, spending the night together!"

"Oh, no..." James looked very embarrassed. "That wasn't what I meant—"

"That's okay. No need to give me the sordid details," said Pomona with a huge grin.

"No, no!" said Caitlyn. Her face was flaming now and she didn't dare look at James. "Pomie, you've completely misunderstood! James meant after he and the police left—after they *questioned me about the murder*!"

"Oh." The disappointment on Pomona's face would have been comical if Caitlyn hadn't been so mortified.

James cleared his throat. "Yes, well... as I said, I'd better be going... I'll... er... look forward to seeing you later tonight."

CHAPTER ELEVEN

After James had left on Arion, with Bran still ambling placidly behind them, Caitlyn helped Pomona gather her mountain of luggage from the car and start across the village to Bertha's cottage. On the way, she filled Pomona in on the rest of the details of the murder, although for some reason, she kept the discovery of the rhinestone, as well as her unease about Evie's behaviour, to herself. *It's not because I really suspect Evie of anything*, she told herself hastily. It was just easier to keep things simple for the time being.

"A real-life love potion!" said Pomona, her eyes sparking with excitement. "Omigod, Caitlyn, that is so cool! I've gotta taste some of this chocolate sauce... speaking of which, how's the chocolate shop doing? Is business better?"

"A bit," said Caitlyn. "There's still a long way to go, but it's a lot better than it was. Yesterday was a great day because a tour coach stopped in the village and a bunch of tourists found the shop. We actually had eight people in the store at one time!" She beamed at Pomona. "Your window display idea is brilliant—if people make it down to the back of the village and the bottom of that lane, and if they see the shop window, then there's a good chance they'll come in. Especially if they smell the gorgeous chocolate aroma wafting out the door! And I told the Widow Mags about your idea of having some tables and chairs in the shop, and she agreed. So we've got those now and they're working great. You were right—once people come in and have a hot chocolate or a piece of cake, they're more likely to buy some chocolate truffles or treats to take home."

"Told you," said Pomona with a smug smile.

"But the problem is getting people down to the back of the village in the first place. Yesterday was a fluke. The chocolate shop is just too hard for a lot of tourists to find. And most of the locals still won't set foot in it, of course," Caitlyn added sadly.

"Stupid morons," Pomona muttered. "How can they not come when the chocolate is so delicious?"

"Well, that's sort of the problem, isn't it? The chocolate is a bit *too* delicious—it tastes so amazing and makes them feel such incredible sensations, people think it must be bewitched."

"Well, maybe they're not wrong," said Pomona

with a grin. "I mean, if the Widow Mags is, like, adding love potions to her chocolate sauce, who knows what she adds to the other chocolate stuff."

"She doesn't add anything other than the best ingredients!" said Caitlyn hotly. "I know—I've seen her make them. She's just a very skilled chocolatier. And that chocolate sauce was a special batch. I think she made it in honour of Midsummer."

"Hey, I don't have a problem with her adding anything," said Pomona, smirking and holding her hands up in mock surrender. "As far as I'm concerned, the Widow Mags can add as many illegal magical substances as she likes! Hey, do you think she could, like, make a Slimming Potion and add it to some chocolates? Then instead of people feeling in love, they'd just get thinner when they ate those chocolates. Hah! I bet they'd be lining up to buy those then, bewitched or not! And you could—"

She broke off as her attention was caught by something in the window of a shop they were passing. Caitlyn, who had walked a few steps ahead, stopped and turned back. She realised that Pomona was gazing at the window of the dress boutique that belonged to Angela Skinner.

"That dress is *gorgeous*! I've got to find out if they have it in my size!" cried Pomona, hurrying into the store.

Caitlyn groaned inwardly. Angela was the last person she wanted to meet, if she could help it. The arrogant young woman had made no secret of her contempt of the Widow Mags and the chocolate shop. And she was still furious at being humiliated when she had tried to vandalise *Bewitched by Chocolate* and ended up with chocolate warts all over her skin, not to mention the time her cheap chocolate drink exploded in her face and covered her in a sticky brown slime... she gave Caitlyn venomous looks whenever they passed in the village

Still... As Caitlyn walked up to the window display and looked at the elegant outfits on the mannequins, she had to admit that Angela had fantastic taste. She herself had bought a dress here recently which was stunning—when she could fit into it, Caitlyn reminded herself sourly, still annoyed for being stupid enough to trust Angela. Her mouth tightened at the memory of the mean trick the other woman had played on her.

She peered into the doorway of the boutique, hoping to grab Pomona and drag her out, but from her cousin's rapt expression as she rifled through a rack of dresses near the door, it looked like a lost cause. Pomona had been bitten by the shopping bug and Caitlyn knew from past experience that the infection was likely to last some time. With a sigh, she followed her cousin into the boutique. As she looked warily around for Angela, she was surprised to find the shop empty. Leaving Pomona still exclaiming excitedly over the dresses on the rack, Caitlyn drifted to the back of the shop, wondering where Angela was. It seemed strange that the other woman would leave the store unattended.

At the back of the long, narrow boutique, she found a door which led to the cramped changing room, and another next to it which was slightly open. A draught of cool air issued from the gap, suggesting that this door connected to the outdoors. Caitlyn hesitated, then pushed the door gently. It swung open and she stepped through, finding herself in a short hallway. An open doorway on her left showed a large room with the remnants of some old kitchen units along one wall and a sink in the corner. Most of the room was taken up with racks of dresses, covered in plastic, and cardboard boxes piled high. Like the Widow Mags's cottage which housed the chocolate shop, the front rooms of this cottage must have been knocked together and converted into the dress boutique, whilst the old kitchen here at the back was being used as a sort of storeroom.

There was another door at the other end of the short hallway, also slightly ajar, with daylight showing clearly through the gap and a strong draught of fresh air blowing through. *It must lead to the alleyway behind the store*, Caitlyn realised. Angela must have popped outside for some reason, and a moment later she heard the other woman's distinct nasal tones:

"...we were all wondering where you were. You never turned up last night!"

"Sorry... real sick... stayed in my room all

night..." came a sullen reply. The voice was so low and muffled that Caitlyn had to strain to make out the words. She tiptoed a few steps closer to the semi-open door.

"You look okay today." Angela's voice was accusing.

"...passed real quick... have been somethin' I ate, maybe a dodgy prawn cocktail... wasn't the real deal... didn't really matter—"

"Yes, but Midsummer's Eve is only two days away! That was the last practice—"

There came another mumble which Caitlyn couldn't catch.

"Yes, well, you'd better be," said Angela, sounding annoyed. "It's hard enough getting to the stone circle without everybody knowing. And you know we need thirteen for the meetings! If you can't handle the commitment, I'm sure others in the village would jump to take your place—"

"...can handle the commitment! ... been to every meeting so far, haven't I? And... a secret—"

"YEAH, HELLO? ANYONE THERE?"

Caitlyn jumped at the sound of the loud American voice. It was Pomona calling from the front of the cottage. She heard a muffled curse from outside, followed by some shuffling, and then Angela's voice saying irritably:

"I've got a customer—I've got to get back. See you later."

Suddenly, Caitlyn realised that she was standing

in the middle of the hallway, in full view of anyone who walked in from the rear alley. She barely had time to whip around and duck into the old kitchen before the back door opened and Angela stepped in. Caitlyn crouched down behind a tower of cardboard boxes and held her breath as she heard the creak of the back door closing, then Angela's rapid footsteps walking past. A minute later, she heard the other woman going through the connecting door, back into the boutique.

Letting her breath out slowly, Caitlyn straightened up and tiptoed out of the kitchen. She hesitated behind the connecting door, not wanting Angela to see her slipping back into the boutique. She could hear the sound of female voices talking, faint and distant. Carefully, she opened the connecting door a crack and peered out. She saw with relief that Angela and Pomona were standing beside a rack next to the front door, at the other end of the boutique. Quickly, she darted through the connecting door and shut it behind her. Then she grabbed a dress at random and stepped into the changing room.

When Angela walked to the back of the boutique a moment later, with Pomona at her heels, Caitlyn was just stepping casually out of the changing room.

"You!" Angela stopped short. "What are you doing here?"

Caitlyn gave the other woman an innocent smile.

"What do you mean? I'm shopping with my cousin."

"I didn't see you in the store when I came in just now." Angela gave her a suspicious look.

"I was in the changing room, trying this on." Caitlyn indicated the dress she was holding.

Angela narrowed her eyes and Caitlyn silently prayed that she hadn't grabbed an XS size from the rack.

"Oh, that's not your colour, Caitlyn," said Pomona from behind Angela. "I told you—redheads shouldn't wear pastel yellow. It makes you look totally washed out."

"Yes, absolutely," said Angela, looking at Pomona with new respect. "I told her that the last time she came in here. And that print too—oh no, not with her hips..."

Caitlyn glanced self-consciously at the nearby mirror, wishing for the hundredth time that she hadn't been "blessed" with a pear-shaped figure. Not that having big hips seemed to bother Pomona in the least, she thought wistfully as she watched her cousin snag a tight denim skirt from a nearby rack. But then, Pomona had the kind of confidence that could pull off a dress made of black rubbish sacks.

Still, at least Angela had been safely distracted and she was kept busy for the next twenty minutes as Pomona tried on practically half the store. By the time they left, laden with several bags, Caitlyn was sure that Angela had forgotten all about the little episode, too busy happily counting her earnings.

Pomona, however, obviously hadn't. She eyed Caitlyn curiously and asked, "Where did you go off to? You weren't really trying on that dress, were you? I knew you'd never wear anything that low-cut."

Quickly, Caitlyn told Pomona about the conversation she had overheard.

"Thirteen for the meetings?" mused Pomona. "It sounds like they're talking about a coven!"

"A what?"

"A coven—a gathering of witches. There are usually thirteen members."

"But Angela wouldn't be part of a coven!" cried Caitlyn. "She hates witches! I've heard her... the way she talks about the Widow Mags and is always jeering at her... and she's accused me of practising witchcraft on her too—"

Pomona shrugged. "Maybe she's really jealous of you. People get like that sometimes—you know, they pretend to hate the thing they really wanna be. It's, like, sour grapes."

Caitlyn shook her head. "But... but why would Angela want to be a witch?"

"For fun? I mean, it's kinda trendy these days to dabble in witchcraft and say you're a 'witch'. My friends back in Hollywood do it; actually, one of them started a coven too. She invited me to join."

"You never told me!" Caitlyn stared at her cousin.

"This was a few months ago. I knew you always scoffed at magic stuff so I didn't bother to mention it." Pomona chuckled. "Kinda ironic, don't you think? The way you never believed in magic and the paranormal—and now you find out that you're a *real* witch?"

"So did you go to this... this coven?"

"Yeah, I went along to one meeting."

"What did you do?"

Pomona giggled. "Oh, you know—burned scented candles, played tarot cards, read each other's horoscopes, messed around with a Ouija board..."

"That's not real witchcraft!" said Caitlyn in disgust.

"Yeah, well, we didn't know, did we?" said Pomona with a laugh. "And anyway, I think most people like the idea of playing around with magic more than really doing it. Like, I think they'd be freaked out if they saw some real magic—but getting all dressed up and pretending you're a witch who can make a love spell to get some guy to notice you... that kinda stuff is sorta cool. I'll bet that's what Angela and her friends are up to."

"I can't believe she's been going around accusing me and the Widow Mags of evil witchcraft and badmouthing us, when she's trying to be a witch herself. What disgusting hypocrisy!" said Caitlyn. Then she gave a gasp. "Pomie, I just remembered: Angela mentioned the stone circle... The bonfires I've been seeing on the hill—that's them, isn't it?"

"Oh yeah—an ancient site like that, associated with myths and legends—that would be, like, *perfect* for a coven meeting. I bet they get a thrill out of thinking they might be summoning up demons or something."

But Caitlyn wasn't listening. She was thinking of something else. "When I first arrived in the village, I went into the post office shop and all the women clammed up when I started asking about the bonfire on the hill... They all said they didn't know anything about it. I bet they were lying! *This* must be why women in the village always pretend the bonfires don't exist and don't comment on it. It's because a lot of them are probably in the coven—or want to be—and don't want to admit it." She paused, frowning. "But... I don't understand. Why are they trying so hard to hide it? I mean, if they think witchcraft is okay—and they must do, otherwise they wouldn't be dabbling in it—then why all the secrecy?"

"Oh, come on, Caitlyn, that's obvious," said Pomona impatiently. "You said it yourself: they're big, fat hypocrites and they don't want everybody to see that. It's like... what's that expression? They wanna have their cake and eat it too. They wanna keep feeling all self-righteous and dissing the Widow Mags and blaming her for stuff—but they also wanna have some fun and mess around with magic themselves."

CHAPTER TWELVE

As it was, the Widow Mags and Bertha both declined James Fitzroy's invitation, and Evie was too shy to come on her own, so it was just Caitlyn and Pomona who set out for Huntingdon Manor that evening in Pomona's red convertible.

"I'm confused—is Nibs, like, living with you at the chocolate shop now? Or with James at the Manor?" asked Pomona, glancing across at the little black kitten who was sitting on Caitlyn's lap, looking wide-eyed at the scenery flashing past.

"I suppose we're sort of sharing," said Caitlyn. "He spends some time with me and the Widow Mags, and then goes back to the Manor for a few days. I know Bran misses him terribly when he's not there and mopes around the house looking for his little friend. But I think the Widow Mags would mope if Nibs stayed at the Manor full-time!" Caitlyn laughed. "It's ironic, you know. She was so against the kitten the first time she saw him—"

"Yeah, I remember—I was there. She nearly snapped our heads off." Pomona chuckled.

"Yes, but I'm starting to learn that her bark is a lot worse than her bite," said Caitlyn with a smile.

"Is it weird to think of her as your grandmother?"

"A bit," Caitlyn admitted. "I mean, it's only been about a week since I found out, so I suppose I'm still getting used to the idea. And she's not exactly the sort of sweet, cuddly old lady type of grandmother either," she said with a dry look.

"You can say that again!" Pomona laughed. Then she sobered and said, "Have you had a chance to ask her about your mother again?"

Caitlyn shook her head. "To be honest, I haven't tried. I have a feeling I won't get anywhere if I keep pushing her now—better to let it rest for a bit until she lets her guard down. Maybe if she gets to know me better... and trusts me... then she might be more willing to talk."

"Hmm... what about Bertha? Wouldn't she know? She's got the same runestone necklace that you have, doesn't she?"

Caitlyn's hand went involuntarily to the stone pendant that she wore around her neck, tucked out of sight beneath her shirt. She ran her fingers over the stone, absently tracing the symbols carved on the surface. The runestone had been around her neck when she had been found as a baby and she had always wondered about its significance. It was one of the things she had come to Tillyhenge in search of answers for—and one of the things that still remained a mystery.

"I don't know... and I sort of feel bad pushing Bertha too much. She's obviously under pressure from the Widow Mags not to talk about it—whatever it is," Caitlyn said.

"Well, there's no rush," said Pomona with a shrug. "It's not like you need to get a job or anything—you've got the money from Aunt Barbara's estate and the royalties from her albums. Are you gonna sell her house back in L.A. though? I mean, if you're planning to remain in England..."

"I don't know," said Caitlyn with a sigh. "I suppose I'll have to make a decision at some point... right now I'm just taking each day as it comes. Maybe I'll make a trip back to the States at the end of summer."

"Maybe you'll be planning to move into a new home by the end of summer," said Pomona with a suggestive smile.

"What's that supposed to mean?"

"Nothing!" Pomona said, giving her a look of exaggerated innocence and turning her attention back to the road.

They had arrived at the entrance to the Huntingdon Manor parklands—two massive stone pillars, each with a stone stag on top, on either side of an ornate wrought-iron gate—and drove smoothly into the dappled avenue, flanked on either side by mature elm trees. Although it was nearly eight-thirty, with it being the height of summer and the days being so long, it was still light as they pulled up the sweeping gravel driveway which curved around the front of the elegant Georgian mansion. In fact, there was a magnificent sun just beginning to set over the Manor, turning the sky into a glorious medley of pinks and oranges.

Pomona gave an exclamation as she got out of the car. "Look at that sky! I gotta get a picture..." She pulled out her phone and held it up, then frowned. "Hmm... the house is too close. I really need to take it from the other side of the lawn to get the whole view..."

She gestured to the wide expanse of manicured lawn in front of them, which started from the edge of the gravel driveway and rolled away from the front of the Manor to merge into the landscaped grounds beyond. "C'mon—let's take a walk down there. We can get a selfie with the Manor and the sky in the background."

"You go first—I'm going to take Nibs into the house," said Caitlyn. "Just to make sure he's left somewhere safe. I'll catch you up."

Pomona nodded and wandered off across the lawn. Caitlyn started up the front steps, then paused as she heard the sound of heavy paws. She turned and saw a huge shape come around the side of the Manor and lumber towards her. It was Bran;

the enormous English mastiff was wagging his tail excitedly as he bounded up to her.

"Hi Bran—I've brought your little friend back," said Caitlyn, showing him Nibs.

"*Meew!*" cried the kitten, wriggling excitedly in her arms to see his canine friend.

Bran shoved his big, baggy face at the kitten, sniffing enthusiastically and headbutting Caitlyn in the process.

"Oomph!" gasped Caitlyn, doubling over. Her hands slipped and she let go of the kitten, who landed on the ground and promptly scampered off.

"Nibs!" Caitlyn regained her balance and dashed after the kitten. "Argh! Come back here!"

The kitten ignored her and disappeared around the side of the Manor. Caitlyn hurried after him, with Bran lumbering happily behind her. She got to the corner just in time to see Nibs's little black tail whisk out of sight through an archway ahead. She rushed after him to find herself in a walled garden which ran down the length of the Manor. There was another archway at the other end of the walled garden and she saw Nibs pause in front of it. He sat down and looked innocently back at her.

Caitlyn approached him slowly, saying in a coaxing voice: "Here, kitty... kitty... kitty... Come on, Nibs..."

"*Meew!*" said Nibs, waiting until she was almost beside him, then jumping up again and scampering through the archway, disappearing into the garden beyond.

Cheeky monkey! He's playing a game and taunting me on purpose! Caitlyn thought irritably. For a moment, she was tempted to abandon the chase. But she knew that James was keen to keep Nibs indoors after dark and she didn't like the thought of leaving the little kitten out alone in the grounds of the huge estate.

She went through the second archway and found herself this time in a more overgrown garden, a forgotten corner tucked in close to the back of the main house. Caitlyn frowned as she looked up at the imposing façade of the Manor rising on her left and wondered which part of the house it corresponded to. She didn't think she had ever been to this side of the Manor. Then a noise drew her attention and she turned to see Bran standing at the base of an ash tree growing beside the house. He was looking up and whining, wagging his tail in a slightly anxious manner. Caitlyn followed his gaze and her heart sank as she saw a little ball of black fur clinging to the tree trunk, high above her head.

"*Nibs!* What are you doing—come down here!"

She rushed to the foot of the tree and strained her eyes to see the little cat properly. The light was beginning to fade now and it was hard to see a black kitten against the dark silhouette of the tree. Only his big yellow eyes shone down at her. She wondered if Nibs had ever tried to climb a tree before—this might have been the first time the kitten had decided to attempt the feat. Well, it looked like he had bitten off more than he could chew! He was too high up now to jump to the ground and the lower section of the trunk was bare of branches, so he couldn't use them as "stepping stones" to move back down the levels. He clung helplessly to the tree trunk, his tiny claws digging into the bark, as he cried for help.

"*Meew!*" he wailed, looking down over his shoulder at her and Bran.

"Hang on, Nibs!" called Caitlyn. "I'll go find a ladder or—wait, what are you doing? No! No, don't go higher!" She watched in dismay as the kitten climbed even higher up the trunk, then crawled out onto a branch. "No… Nibs, don't walk out on that!"

Caitlyn watched, her heart pounding now, as the kitten—balancing precariously on the branch—walked towards its tapering tip. Bran whined, pacing around the tree. The branch swayed alarmingly and Caitlyn was sure that the kitten would fall off. She was wondering wildly if she would be able to catch him if he fell, when she saw that the branch stretched towards the Manor and one of the upper windows. She held her breath as the kitten negotiated the last stretch of wobbling wood, then exhaled in relief as Nibs jumped off the branch and onto the safety of the window ledge.

"Okay, stay there, Nibs! Stay there!" she called to the kitten, who had started to pace up and down the ledge, crying and eyeing the ground below.

"Whatever you do, don't jump!"

Caitlyn looked frantically around, wishing she knew enough magic to help in this situation. But nothing she had learned so far came anywhere near the ability to make the kitten float down to the ground—or herself fly up to reach him. She wouldn't know where to start, and even if she did, she wouldn't dare try it. The risk of messing up and hurting the kitten or herself was too great.

She would have to do things the ordinary, mundane way: with a ladder. But where was the quickest place to get a ladder? She would have to run back to the front of the Manor—a long way now—or to the rear service entrance, which was farther around this side of the building, to find someone who could get the equipment for her. She shot a worried look up at the crying kitten. Would Nibs stay on the window ledge while she was gone? She was terrified at the thought of coming back to find a crumpled kitten on the ground beneath the window.

Then she spied the door. It was partly concealed behind a bush, so that she had almost missed it. If she could get into the house, she might be able to open the upstairs window to rescue Nibs. She rushed up to the door but her heart sank as she gave the door handle a tug and it held fast. Of course, it would be locked. Then a memory flashed in her mind of the Widow Mags waving a hand over the stillroom cupboard, muttering: "*Aperio!*"—and the door swinging open. Without even stopping to think, Caitlyn raised her own hand and stared at the door handle, concentrating hard.

"*Aperio!*"

To her surprised delight, there was a loud *click* and the door swung open with a rusty creak. She stepped inside and found herself in a darkened hallway leading into the Manor. But the thing which drew her eye was a wide doorway to the right, which gave onto a stairwell. In a flash, Caitlyn was running up the old wooden staircase, which zigzagged up to the upper floor. She came out into another darkened hallway and paused for a moment, trying to get her bearings. She spied a window nearby and hurried over, peering out to see where she was in relation to the tree outside.

Almost instantly, she saw Nibs. His window ledge was the next one along, and Caitlyn realised that it could be accessed via the room next to her. She turned from the window and surveyed the door to the room: a thick oak affair, heavily studded, with a brass ring pull for a doorknob—like something out of a medieval dungeon. As she reached for the ring, she said, without even thinking, *"Aperio!"* She felt a surge of delighted surprise again as she heard another loud *click* and the heavy door opened with a faint creak.

Caitlyn stepped inside, hesitating on the threshold. It was a much larger room than she had expected, long and narrow and running the length of the house. There were oil portraits hanging on the walls and various pieces of furniture scattered about, all covered in white sheets. There was a cloying smell of mould and decay, and the air lay heavily in the room, as if no one had come in here for a very long time. Caitlyn glanced uneasily around as she crossed the room to the nearest window, her steps leaving footprints on the dusty wooden floor. She didn't have time to look properly but she caught a fleeting glimpse of faces, with eyes which seemed to follow her, looking out from the ornate gilt frames on the walls.

Then she was at the window, peering out anxiously for any sign of a little black kitten. It was a relief to draw back the velvet curtains and see him there, on the other side of the pane of glass, trembling on the ledge. Caitlyn undid the latch. It was a heavy sash window which had not been opened for a very long time, so it was stiff in its frame and took a massive effort for her to shove the lower section upwards. It heaved open with a screech like a banshee and the kitten jumped in terror, his black fur standing on end, his yellow eyes enormous.

"No—wait, Nibs... it's me! *Don't jump!*" Caitlyn screamed.

She lunged through the open window, reaching for the kitten, but it was too late. Nibs had flung himself off the ledge and plummeted down to the ground.

CHAPTER THIRTEEN

"NIBS!"

Caitlyn leaned over the windowsill, hardly daring to look down. Her heart, which had leapt into her throat, slowly returned to its rightful place in her chest as she saw the large bush beneath the window which had cushioned the kitten's landing. Nibs was lying, stunned, in a tangle of broken leaves and stems, but as she watched, he began to struggle feebly and she breathed a huge sigh of relief.

Shutting the window, Caitlyn hurried out of the room, pulling the heavy door shut behind her, and ran back down the stairs. She rushed outside and over to the bush, reaching up to disentangle the kitten and lift him down. She held him in her arms and examined him carefully, glad to see that he didn't jerk away or cry out in pain as she prodded him all over

"Meew..." said Nibs, starting to wriggle in her grasp.

"Yes, well, you're lucky you didn't break anything," said Caitlyn crossly. She set him down for a second on the ground, just to make sure that he could stand properly, then quickly scooped him up again before he could run off. "Come on, no more adventures for you tonight!"

She looked around for Bran but the mastiff was nowhere in sight. She wondered if he had gone off to find James and get help. In any case, twilight was starting to fall in earnest now and she didn't want to stand here in this overgrown garden, waiting for the dog in the gathering dark. She was sure she would see him and James if she headed back around to the front of the Manor.

Carrying the kitten against her chest, Caitlyn stepped out of the overgrown garden and into the wide avenue that encircled the main house. It was bordered on either side by a tall hedge, almost like a path in a maze. But unlike a maze, the hedge walls had little alcoves cut into them at short intervals, each hosting a carved stone bench or classical statue. The overall effect was picturesque and elegant, like walking through a living art gallery.

Caitlyn hadn't gone several paces when she heard someone on the other side of the hedge. Her feet slowed as she recognised the voices. One was

Inspector Walsh... and the other—a nervous, young male voice—belonged to Chris Bottom.

"... no, I told you—I didn't see her again after I dropped her off at her house!"

"Very well, very well. Now, going back to when you dropped Mandy off... Did you see anything strange—anyone loitering about the place?"

"Well, I've been thinking about that and I do remember..." Chris paused. "I did see this weird old bloke."

"Yes?" said Inspector Walsh sharply.

"Meew!"

Nibs squirmed in Caitlyn's arms. She shushed the baby cat, tucking him into the crook of her elbow. He seemed to like this position better and settled down, purring softly. Caitlyn glanced back at the hedge, hoping that they hadn't heard the kitten's cry. To her relief, it sounded like the questioning had continued uninterrupted.

"...strange man loitering around Miss Harper's house?"

"Well, not her house exactly. He was loitering around my bike."

"Your bicycle?"

"Yeah. Like I told you, Mandy got me to go in with her 'cos she wanted to show me her economics project, and I had to leave my bike out by the front gate. When I came back out, there was this old bloke there fiddling with the box of chocolates."

"These were the chocolates you were delivering to

the Manor?"

"Yeah, the samples from the Widow Mags. I was going to come straight back to the Manor, see, but Mandy asked me to give her a lift—"

"Yes, yes, you said. Go on. So the old man was 'fiddling' with the box?"

"Well, he'd opened the box and was sort o' looking inside. I dunno what he was doing. Anyway, I hollered at him and he dropped the box and scarpered."

"What did he look like? Would you recognise him again?"

"Oh yeah," said Chris with conviction. "Won't forget him in a hurry. He looked really ancient. And he was wearing one of those funny black suits—you know, like in them BBC dramas that my aunt likes to watch. With Colin Firth. When he comes out of the lake and all."

"Ah... you mean like Pride and Prejudice? A period costume drama?"

"Yeah. That's the one. Same kind of black jacket—and the funny shirts with the high collars. He spoke funny too."

The description sounded suspiciously like Viktor. Caitlyn wondered what on earth the old vampire had been doing with the box of chocolates. Probably just being nosy, as usual. Viktor seemed to spend an inordinate amount of time meandering around Tillyhenge and the Manor, wandering into places he shouldn't.

"...did he look dangerous to you?"

"I dunno about dangerous," said Chris doubtfully. "Like I said, he looked really old."

"Did you see where he went?"

There was a moment's hesitation. "Not really. It was a bit weird, actually. I looked down to check the chocolates—in case he'd nicked any—and then when I looked up again, he was gone. It was like he just disappeared."

"Nobody just disappears," said Inspector Walsh impatiently.

"Well, he did," insisted Chris. "I could see all the way down the lane and around the field—couldn't see the old bloke anywhere. Dunno where he could have gone. Even if he had been walking fast, I would have seen him in the distance. Unless he flew away or something." He laughed.

"Hmm... well, thank you, Mr Bottom. You've been very helpful."

"Can I go now?"

"Yes, although we may need to speak to you again."

There was a rustle behind the hedge and Caitlyn hurriedly stepped back. She didn't want Inspector Walsh to find her eavesdropping. She could see that there was a gap in the hedge ahead and had a suspicion that it was a connecting doorway. The inspector might be coming that way. She looked around wildly and ducked into the nearest alcove. A stone bench had been set there, probably a couple of centuries ago from the look of the worn corners and lichen growing across its surface. Caitlyn sat down gingerly on the edge of the bench and cuddled Nibs closer to her, hoping that the kitten would stay quiet.

There was more rustling and then, a moment later, she heard Inspector Walsh's voice, accompanied by a respectful "Yes, sir." She peeked out of her alcove to see that her hunch had been right: the detective had used the cut-through and was now in the avenue ahead of her, heading back towards the front of the Manor, with a young constable at his side. She watched their retreating backs, waiting until they were small figures in the distance before she stepped out of the alcove. But just as she started down the avenue again, she bumped into someone else coming through the gap.

"Chris!" she said in surprise. "I thought you'd left—I mean, er...."

The boy had a preoccupied expression and didn't seem to notice her odd greeting.

"Oh, hi," he said absently. "You looking for Lord Fitzroy?"

"Er... Sort of. I was actually chasing after Nibs. He ran up a tree and then got stuck on a window ledge."

Chris's face softened as he saw the kitten clutched in Caitlyn's arms. "Yeah, he's a right little monkey, that one," he said with a chuckle, reaching out to pat the kitten on the head.

"So, um..." Caitlyn gave him a casual sideways glance. "Have the police been questioning you about Mandy?"

The smile left his face. He nodded soberly. "Can't believe she's dead," he mumbled, bewilderment in his candid brown eyes. "I mean, I was only speaking to her yesterday."

"Did you know her well?" asked Caitlyn gently.

Chris shrugged. "I suppose... We were in the same class at school and she was always talking to me and stuff..." He looked down, blushing slightly.

"Did she talk to you yesterday? I mean, did she say anything that might—"

"The police asked me that." He hesitated, giving her an uncertain look.

"Yes?"

He ducked his head, muttering, "Nothing."

Caitlyn had the impression that he had something he desperately wanted to get off his chest. But she could see from the way he was eyeing her that he wasn't sure whether to trust her. After all, he hardly knew her—there was no reason for him to confide in her.

On an impulse, she put a hand on his arm and said gently, "You can trust me, Chris. I won't repeat anything you say."

The boy hesitated again, then blurted: "There was something I didn't tell Inspector Walsh."

"Yes?"

He shifted uncomfortably. "It's... it's not nice to

speak ill of the dead. But… but I don't know if it might be important…"

Caitlyn gave him an encouraging smile. "Maybe if you tell me, I can help you decide if it's relevant?"

"Yeah," he said, looking relieved. "Yeah, that's a good idea."

"So… Mandy said something?" Caitlyn prompted.

"It wasn't something she said, exactly… it was more something she was planning to do." He gave her a slightly ashamed look. "It was about Evie."

"About Evie?" said Caitlyn, surprised.

"Yeah. Mandy was laughing and saying some bitc—oops, sorry! I mean, some rude things about Evie, you know, like how she looked and dressed… and about her mother, Bertha… And then she said she was planning to go to Evie's place that night… Last night, I mean."

"To do what?"

He shrugged. "Dunno exactly. She wouldn't tell me…" He shifted uncomfortably again. "I don't reckon it was something nice. She… she could be pretty mean sometimes, Mandy."

Caitlyn stared at him, her mind whirling. What had Mandy Harper been planning to do to Evie last night? And if she had planned to go to Evie's house, how had she ended up behind the Widow Mags's cottage?

"Do you think I need to tell Inspector Walsh?" Chris looked at her anxiously.

Caitlyn hesitated. Part of her wanted to say no,

so that Evie wouldn't be dragged into the murder investigation any more than necessary. But another part of her knew that they couldn't keep this from the police, especially as this gave new information about Mandy's whereabouts on the night of her murder.

"Yes, I think so," she said with a sigh. "It might have nothing to do with Mandy's murder but... I suppose the police ought to know everything, just in case." Then she added quickly, "But Inspector Walsh has probably finished for the day now. I'm sure it'll be fine if you speak to him tomorrow."

This will give me time to speak to Evie first, Caitlyn thought, and warn her about the police's impending questions.

Chris nodded and, looking grateful, bade her goodbye, heading in the opposite direction, back down the avenue and towards the rear of the property. Caitlyn watched him go for a moment, then glanced down at her arms. Nibs had been very quiet and now she could see why: the little kitten had fallen asleep! That adventure with the tree and the window ledge must have worn him out. He was curled up against her now, comfortably nestled in the crook of her arm with his tiny paws tucked against his chest and his whiskers curled around his face. She felt her heart melt slightly at the sight of him.

Cradling him closer, she turned and headed slowly back towards the front of the Manor. But she hadn't gone far when she saw a tall figure hurrying towards her, accompanied by a four-legged form the size of a small pony.

"Caitlyn! Are you all right? Bran came to find me and he was frantic about something, whining and drooling and pulling at my clothing. I finally realised he wanted me to follow him—"

"It's all right—it was Nibs. He was stuck up in a tree, but I got him down, and he's safe and sound." Caitlyn bent down to show the kitten to the big dog, who was sniffing anxiously around her. "Here you go, Bran—see? Nibs is fine! But you're a good boy to go and get help."

"WOOF!" The mastiff wagged his tail joyously and gave her a soggy slurp with his huge pink tongue, leaving a trail of dog drool on her cheek.

"Ugh!" Caitlyn straightened up again, scrubbing her face with one hand.

"Oh, sorry!" said James. He pulled a crisp white handkerchief out of his pocket and handed it to her. "Here..."

Here we go again, thought Caitlyn wryly. If she managed to spend an hour in James Fitzroy's company without taking yet another handkerchief off him, it would be a miracle.

"Thanks," she said. "Have you seen Pomona, by the way? I just remembered that I left her wandering around the front lawns. I told her I'd join her right away; she must be getting worried—"

"Not to worry, I found her. We've been having

drinks in the Conservatory. She was getting a bit concerned though—we both were—so she'll be glad to see you." As he spoke, James began escorting her towards the front of the house. "Did you say Nibs was stuck in a tree?"

Caitlyn sighed. "Yes, I was bringing him into the house and lost hold of him, and then he ran off—I think he was playing a game and trying to get me to chase him. Anyway, he went up a tree and probably climbed a bit higher than he meant to... I really need to get a proper cat carrier for him, so that he can travel safely when we move him back and forth between here and the chocolate shop." She blushed slightly as she said "we"—somehow, it always felt a bit intimate when they discussed their joint ownership of the kitten they had rescued together, although she knew that it was probably just her own silly, overactive imagination.

James frowned thoughtfully. "Yes, I did have a look in the stables a few days ago but we don't have anything suitable."

"I asked in the village post shop but they said I would have to go to a proper pet store in one of the nearby market towns."

"I can pick one up, if you like, the next time I—"

"No," said Caitlyn. "No, I found the kitten, really, so he's more my responsibility. I'll get the carrier and I—"

She broke off. They had just walked around the side of the house and she saw two men coming down the front steps of the Manor: Inspector Walsh and one of his constables.

"Ah, Miss Le Fey—how fortunate to see you here," said the inspector. "I have some further questions for you. I realise it is dinner time but if you could spare me a few moments...?"

His tone was perfectly courteous but Caitlyn noticed a grim expression in his eyes. She glanced at James. He nodded and reached out to take the kitten from her arms.

"Certainly, Inspector. We'll wait for Caitlyn in the Conservatory. Come, Bran!"

He strode into the house, with the mastiff at his heels, whilst Caitlyn turned apprehensively to follow the detective. What could he want to question her about?

CHAPTER FOURTEEN

"So... um... have you had the autopsy report back yet?" asked Caitlyn as she followed Inspector Walsh to the nearby police car. "Do they know how Mandy was killed?"

The inspector leaned against the bonnet of the car and regarded her for a moment, as if debating whether to tell her, then gave a slight shrug, acknowledging that the news would be travelling around the village soon anyway.

"Yes, the forensic pathologist's guess was right. Mandy Harper died from a blow to the head."

"I don't remember seeing any injury to her head," said Caitlyn, frowning.

"It was a closed head wound—there was no external injury but there was a significant impact to the skull. This in itself wouldn't normally have killed her but the pathologist found that Mandy had a congenital brain aneurysm—a sort of enlarged blood bubble, if you like, in one of the vessels in her brain," he explained. "When she fell backwards, she smacked her head on a sharp rock which fractured her skull and burst the aneurysm. She would have felt very little pain," he added quickly, seeing Caitlyn's expression of horror.

"Does this mean it's going to be harder to find out who killed her, since there's no weapon?"

"Yes, strictly speaking, she was killed by a rock on the ground," said Inspector Walsh. "But I suppose you could say that the person who pushed her was the murderer. Someone who shoved her with enough force so that she fell over and smacked her head on the rock."

"So it could have been an accident?"

"Yes, it could have been an accident. However, it's not likely. There are signs of a struggle: the scratches on her face and the bruises… it would seem that Mandy Harper was fighting with someone before she died."

"Someone who wanted the vial of love potion and was trying to snatch it from her!" cried Caitlyn. "Like Dennis Kirby!"

The inspector's face took on a familiar scornful expression at the mention of the love potion. However, he said grudgingly, "Yes, we are working on the assumption that the murderer wanted something from Mandy and, in the course of the struggle, pushed her over, causing her to fall backwards and hit her head. Considering where she was found and the fact that there were signs of a break-in at the cottage, I think it is also safe to assume that this item was something that was in the Widow Mags's stillroom, probably in the locked cupboard which was found with its door open. Now..." He leaned forwards. "This is what I wanted to ask you about, Miss Le Fey. The Forensics team has found three sets of fresh prints on the cupboard door—that is, three people had touched and opened that door recently. One set belongs to the Widow Mags, the second belongs to Mandy Harper, and the third..." he paused, watching her closely, "...belongs to Evie."

"E-Evie?"

"Yes, the Widow Mags's granddaughter, Evie." He gave her a hard look. "And I have just learned that, apparently, the Widow Mags is your grandmother as well?"

"Yes," Caitlyn said, trying not to sound defensive. "Yes, I only just found out recently myself. The Widow Mags is my maternal grandmother."

"Which makes Bertha your aunt and Evie your cousin," said Inspector Walsh. He narrowed his eyes. "Now, why would her prints be on the cupboard door?"

Caitlyn's mind raced. "Oh... um... it's because she helped the Widow Mags return the love potion. To the cupboard, I mean."

Inspector Walsh raised his eyebrows. "I don't remember the Widow Mags mentioning that."

"She... she probably forgot. She was busy finishing up the chocolate sauce after she added the 'love-in-idleness' extract and... and so Evie helped her seal the vial and put it back in the stillroom."

"I see." Inspector Walsh sat back and gave her an appraising look. Caitlyn had to fight to keep her expression nonchalant under that shrewd gaze. Desperate to distract him, she said, "So... um... have you questioned Dennis Kirby and Professor Ruskin yet?"

"Yes. And they both seem unlikely suspects."

"What do you mean, 'unlikely'?" said Caitlyn indignantly. "They're the most *likely* suspects! Especially Dennis Kirby! He—"

"Mr Kirby has an alibi for the time of the murder," said Inspector Walsh. "The forensic pathologist estimates that Mandy Harper was killed just after midnight and you found her body at around 12:20 a.m. Kirby says he was on the phone, talking to a business associate in Indonesia, from half past eleven until a quarter past midnight—"

"He could be ly—"

"He used the landline in his room at the pub, Miss Le Fey, as he could not get reception on his mobile phone. And we have already asked British Telecom to check their records. They confirm that a call was indeed put through from the village pub to a cocoa plantation in Sulawesi, Indonesia and that the line was engaged between the times of 11:32 p.m. and 12:17 a.m. So it seems that Dennis Kirby was telling the truth—he was talking on the phone, which means that he could not have also been the murderer."

Caitlyn bit her lip. "Okay, what about Professor Ruskin, then? What's his alibi?"

"He says he was asleep. He had a drink with Kirby, then went up to his room at around 11:20 p.m. and went straight to bed."

"Well, if nobody was with him, there's no proof that he was sleeping!"

"There's no proof that he wasn't either," Inspector Walsh said evenly. "Miss Le Fey, regardless of these facts, might I remind you that neither man has any connection to Mandy Harper."

"But I told you, the love potion—"

"That is simply your assumption. In fact, I asked Kirby about the... er... 'love potion' and he says he had simply come to see the Widow Mags about a chocolate sauce recipe. A *normal* chocolate sauce recipe. He denied any knowledge of a 'love potion'."

"He's lying!"

Inspector Walsh raised his eyebrows and Caitlyn flushed.

"Sorry..." she said. "I don't mean to be rude but I... um... happened to speak to Professor Ruskin this morning and he said while they were having drinks together last night, Dennis Kirby was bragging about a love potion and how it was going to 'make him rich'."

"Yes, Professor Ruskin mentioned that to me as well when I questioned him," said Inspector Walsh dryly. "He also mentioned that the Fairy King and Queen are dancing in the forest and that the stone circle is really a giant fairy ring with dangerous powers, which cannot be entered without magical protection… I must say, I wonder about the many poor tourists who have visited the stone circle. Perhaps we should be helping them look for their lost souls?" His tone was dripping with sarcasm now. "I'm sure you can see, Miss Le Fey, why I am not inclined to take much of what Professor Ruskin says as reliable fact. My men have checked his background and it seems that while his imaginative theories regarding Shakespeare are a great source of amusement to his colleagues, his obsession has severely damaged his academic credibility and his university has actually invited him to take 'early retirement', to reduce embarrassment to his department."

Caitlyn digested this in silence.

Inspector Walsh clasped his hands behind him. "The police have limited resources and I will not send my men off on a wild goose chase when there are better avenues for us to explore first. As I said before, neither man is known to have had any contact with the victim. They have not been observed meeting her, speaking to her, or interacting with Mandy in any way. Unless you can tell me different...?" He paused and looked at her.

"No," Caitlyn admitted. "I haven't seen her speaking to either man."

"Then I'm inclined to focus the investigation on Mandy Harper's background. It *is* an established fact that most murder victims knew their killer. My hunch is that the murderer is likely to be someone who had a grudge against Mandy. Now, I have been interviewing staff and students at her school today and I gathered that Mandy, although popular in school, was... shall we say... not the most *charitable* person in Tillyhenge? It wouldn't be surprising if she had a few enemies—perhaps even someone of her own age, who was resentful of the way Mandy had treated her." He paused significantly. "Such as your cousin, Evie?"

Caitlyn stiffened. She made an effort to keep her expression neutral as the inspector regarded her. When she remained silent, he continued:

"We received an anonymous tip-off saying Evie had suffered a lot of bullying at Mandy Harper's hands and had finally snapped. The message said that Evie had killed Mandy in revenge."

"That's a lie!" cried Caitlyn. "Evie would never do anything like that, even if she had been bullied. She's... she's very sweet and gentle. She could never hurt anyone!"

The inspector raised his eyebrows, then said in a casual voice, "The Widow Mags kindly provided us with receipts from all the customers who were in the chocolate shop yesterday and we managed to track down a few of the tourists who were still in the area. One of them had an interesting story to tell us: they recalled an incident in the shop—an incident which you had failed to mention…"

"What do you mean?" asked Caitlyn, licking her lips nervously.

"I understand that when Mandy came into the store, she made some unpleasant comments to Evie and, according to the witness, after Mandy left, Evie was in a state of great anger and agitation and was heard to exclaim—I quote—*'I hate her! I wish Mandy Harper would drop dead!'*" He looked Caitlyn straight in the eye. "That doesn't sound very sweet and gentle to me."

"I… well… that was just letting off steam," said Caitlyn. "I mean, it doesn't mean anything, really. It's the sort of thing you say when you're venting. Everyone does that."

Inspector Walsh's face was grim. "Perhaps… But it is interesting that someone with good reason to have a grudge against Mandy Harper was heard voicing a wish for her death, only a few hours before Mandy was found dead."

CHAPTER FIFTEEN

Caitlyn left her interview with Inspector Walsh feeling quite shaken and was glad that the walk to the Conservatory allowed her time to compose herself before seeing James and Pomona. The last thing she needed was for them to notice her agitation and start asking awkward questions about Evie too.

She found them sitting in a pair of wicker armchairs at one end of the Conservatory, sipping Pimm's and talking and laughing easily. James sprang up when he saw her and said:

"Ah! At last!"

"I'm sorry—you must be starving," said Caitlyn. "You should have started dinner without me."

"Oh, no, we're fine, but I'm concerned about Mrs Pruett having to stay too late. My cook," he explained at Caitlyn's puzzled look. He gave a slightly exasperated smile. "I actually told her that we'd be perfectly happy with some cold meats and cheese and bread, so that she could just leave the things and go home, but she insisted on cooking a full meal and staying to oversee it. Still, at least I've managed to convince her to just put everything on the table, rather than serve several courses. But she's insisted on us eating in the Dining Room," he added, almost apologetically, as he led the way to a room that Caitlyn had never seen before.

She faltered in the doorway, slightly overawed by the stately room, which featured an enormous chandelier above the gleaming mahogany dining table, ornate plasterwork on the ceiling, and a huge mullioned window along one wall, matched by an equally enormous fireplace on the other.

"Holy guacamole!" exclaimed Pomona, standing round-eyed next to Caitlyn on the threshold. "Are we, like, going to have dinner with the Queen?"

"It *is* a bit much, isn't it?" said James, looking around. "When my father was alive, he liked to have dinner in here every night. He was a great stickler for tradition and proper etiquette, whereas I prefer things more down-to-earth and low-key. I do use the Morning Room for breakfast and lunch sometimes, but for the evenings, I usually just have something simple like soup and bread on a tray in my study. It bothers the staff a bit, I think, especially the ones like Mrs Pruett who have been with my family for years. They're used to my father's formal style. For instance, I like to just head down to the kitchen and make myself a mug of tea in the afternoons—which causes Mrs Pruett no amount of indignation." He gave a rueful chuckle. "She wants me to have a full tea service in the Drawing Room, with freshly baked scones, jam, and clotted cream. I suppose I'm used to fending for myself after so many years overseas and it's been a bit of an adjustment on both sides, me coming back to take on the title of 'Lord Fitzroy' at the Manor."

"Maybe they're worried they'll lose their jobs if you don't keep doing things the way your Dad had them?" Pomona suggested.

"I've assured them that their positions are in no danger. Just because I'm not having a three-course meal every evening doesn't mean I'm going to fire Mrs Pruett any time soon," said James. "I've simply found new ways to use her skills. For example, Lisa, my Events Coordinator, has been consulting her on all the refreshment options we offer tourists and the catering we do for weddings and other events. Mrs Pruett is also going to be heavily involved in our plans to convert the coach house into a restaurant. In fact, I've officially changed her title to Catering Manager for the Manor—although, I have to say, she didn't seem very impressed when I told her," he added with another rueful chuckle.

At that moment, a door on the other side of the Dining Room opened and a plump, motherly-looking woman in her late fifties bustled in, carrying a large tureen of soup.

"Master James!" she cried. "What are you standing there for? Let the young ladies sit down!" She set the soup on the table and hurried over, shooing them towards the chairs like a motherly sheepdog.

Caitlyn stared at the assortment of plates and dishes on the table. There was potted shrimp—tiny spiced shrimp preserved in clarified butter—served with crisp, thin slices of toast, split pea soup with smoked ham, baby carrots and asparagus sautéed in butter and—sitting proudly in the centre of the table—a traditional roast lamb, complete with fragrant rosemary, roasted garlic, and a refreshing mint sauce, and accompanied by crispy roast potatoes.

"Mrs Pruett, this is far too much food!" James protested. "I thought we were just having a simple meal—maybe some soup and sandwiches—"

Mrs Pruett looked horrified. "Entertaining young ladies and not providing proper cooking? I don't know what new-fangled ideas you've picked up while gallivanting abroad, Master James, but that's not how we do things in England!" She gave an emphatic nod. "Besides, if you don't make a good impression on the young ladies, how will any of them decide that she might like to stay here permanently?" She gave James a meaningful look and a not-so-subtle glance at Caitlyn and Pomona.

It was obvious that having known James since he was a child, Mrs Pruett—like many of the older members of the staff and residents of the village—had a maternal attitude towards him and a keen interest to see him settled with a wife and a baby to continue the Fitzroy line. The endurance of the Fitzroy family estate had been the bedrock of the Tillyhenge community and surrounding farms for generations—and the idea of a young, single Lord Fitzroy living at the Manor on his own was obviously unsettling.

A faint line of red appeared on James's cheeks. He cleared his throat and said hurriedly, "Um. Yes... *Ahem.* Mrs Pruett, that's really not... Look, I just didn't want to give you too much work. I mean, this all looks delicious but it's meant that you've had to stay late—"

"That's no concern of yours," said Mrs Pruett briskly. She glanced up as the door behind her opened again and a young woman stepped in, carrying a tray of glasses and a bottle of wine, as well as a jug of water. The cook's expression cooled and she said, her tone sharp, "About time, Traci... and you forgot the dessert spoons when you set the table."

"Thought James said they were just goin' to help themselves afterwards?" said the young woman insolently.

"That's *Lord Fitzroy* to you," snapped Mrs Pruett. "And while I'm cook in this house, we'll have a properly-set table."

Traci flounced over to the table and set the tray down with bad grace. Caitlyn watched her curiously. She knew the two maids who worked at the Manor—this girl was a stranger. She was also dressed very differently to the Manor's usual staff. Instead of their elegant, tasteful outfits, this girl was wearing tight black jeans and a tank top which showed a bit too much of her cleavage. Caitlyn saw Mrs Pruett compress her lips with disapproval as she eyed the girl walking around the table, placing the glasses at each setting.

Caitlyn wondered if one of the usual maids had been replaced. She knew that Amelia had been on probation after a (supposedly misguided) attempt to steal a Fitzroy family heirloom. Pomona was obviously thinking the same thing because, as soon as Traci had left the room, she turned to James and said:

"Is that your new maid? Did you fire Amelia?"

"No, that's Traci Duff, the new barmaid down at the village pub," James explained. "She's just filling in for a few days, as Jenny and Amelia are both on holiday and we're a bit short-staffed. It was lucky that Traci was willing to lend a hand and she happens to be staying at a room at the pub, so she can easily come and go."

Mrs Pruett made a harrumphing sound. "Let's hope it won't turn out to be *un*lucky," she muttered with a dark look.

"Whaddya mean?" asked Pomona.

The cook sniffed disapprovingly. "No good will come of hiring those with sticky fingers, you mark my words. We'll be lucky if the silver doesn't go missing—"

"Come on, Mrs Pruett," said James with a patient smile. "You know nothing was ever proven."

"I know what I heard," said the cook stubbornly. She turned to Pomona. "Traci was working at a pub in the next village along before she came to Tillyhenge. My sister lives there and she told me customers were having things nicked from their bags when Traci worked there... it's a disgrace! And she was seen too. A girl saw her sticking her hand in a handbag—told the landlord and he fired Traci immediately." She gave James a fierce look. "Don't know what Terry, our landlord, was thinking, hiring her."

James sighed. "Mrs Pruett—that was all just hearsay. That landlord could have had other reasons for letting Traci go. Remember, he never said it was because he suspected her of theft, whatever the gossips might say. Anyway, I, for one, respect Terry's judgement. If he's happy to keep Traci on at his pub—and even let her sleep there—then that means he trusts her. Which means we should too. Remember, in this country, you're innocent until proven guilty."

Mrs Pruett gave a contemptuous sniff but did not reply. Instead, she made the shooing motion with her hands again and said, "Well, sit down! Sit down! The food is getting cold."

"This looks amazing," Caitlyn said, smiling warmly at the cook as James pulled a chair out for her and seated her at the table.

"Yeah," said Pomona, eyeing the roast lamb hungrily. "I can't wait to pig out on this!"

Mrs Pruett beamed and gave them an approving nod. "There's nothing like a traditional British roast, I always say. Proper, good old-fashioned cooking, with simple ingredients. Not this ridiculous fused cooking and gastric pubs and other nonsense that's everywhere these days." She waved a hand at the two girls. "Well, don't just sit there gawking! Tuck in! Tuck in!"

They began eating under Mrs Pruett's beady eye and the food was so good that there was practically no conversation until everyone had had second helpings.

"Man, I'm going to gain, like, ten pounds after tonight," said Pomona as she sat back at last with a satisfied sigh.

James chuckled. "You haven't even had dessert yet," he said, indicating the glass dish of summer berry trifle that Mrs Pruett had brought in a few minutes ago.

"Oh, no... no dessert for me," moaned Pomona. "Otherwise, I'll be the size of a cow!"

Mention of cows made Caitlyn think of Ferdinand and she asked James if he had seen the bull that afternoon.

"Yes, I arrived at the field just in time to see him approaching the herd to try and make friends again," said James with a grimace. "It didn't go well, poor fellow. He was chased across the field by one of the cows."

Pomona burst out laughing. "But he's a bull, right? He must be, like, much bigger than the cows? He could teach them a lesson if he wanted to."

"I suppose... but he's a lover, not a fighter. That's why they named him Ferdinand," said James with a wry smile.

Pomona held up a forefinger. "You know what you need? A cow whisperer!"

"Well, I'm hoping we might get something similar. The vet rang me this afternoon and told me that he had a colleague who's a bit of a bovine expert. He's going to speak to him and get back to me, maybe even arrange for his colleague to come and see Ferdinand on Monday morning—oh, actually, it'll have to be later because I've got that meeting with Blackmort."

"Blackmort?" Pomona looked up with interest. "You mean Thane Blackmort?"

"Yes, I have a meeting with him first thing Monday morning," James said absently as he reached across to serve Caitlyn some of the berry trifle.

"Oh, no—no, thank you," said Caitlyn quickly.

"Surely you're not on a diet?" said James with a

smile.

Caitlyn flushed. "No, but I probably should be."

"Rubbish," said James with a laugh. "You look fine to me."

Caitlyn's heart skipped a beat. Did James notice her figure? She cleared her throat and said, "I'll... I'll just have a coffee, I think," as she reached hastily for the cafetière of fresh coffee that Mrs Pruett had left on the table.

James snapped his fingers and said, "I just remembered—I haven't had a chance to try those chocolate samples from the Widow Mags yet. We can have them with the coffee. They're in my study—hang on a tick, I'll go and get them."

He returned a few moments later with a familiar-looking cardboard box. The memory of the last time she had seen that box flashed through Caitlyn's mind and, for a moment, it was hard to believe that it had only been yesterday when she had been standing at the counter in *Bewitched by Chocolate*, handing Chris the chocolates, and Mandy Harper had still been alive.

"I'm surprised you need to taste any of them," Pomona laughed. "I can tell you they're all delectable."

James chuckled as he opened the box. The heavenly aroma of rich, decadent chocolate drifted out. "Ah, well, any excuse to taste more of the Widow Mags's creations—"

He broke off and frowned as he peered into the

box. Reaching a hand inside, he lifted two long pale yellow things out and stared at them quizzically. Caitlyn choked on her coffee.

Viktor's fangs!

CHAPTER SIXTEEN

Pomona sat up. "Hey! Are those tee—"

"Oh, I'll take those," said Caitlyn quickly, swiping the fangs out of James's hands. "Sorry, they must have slipped in—they're not meant to be part of the sample batch."

"What are they?" asked James, trying to look in her hands.

"They looked like fangs," said Pomona helpfully.

Caitlyn tried to kick her cousin under the table. "Fangs? Uh... Ha-ha... no, of course not. You must be imagining things. They're just... um... some chocolates that I was... er... making myself. But they're not part of the Widow Mags's selection so you don't want to bother with them—"

"You've been making chocolates yourself, Caitlyn? How cool!" said Pomona. "Let's see!"

Caitlyn groaned inwardly. She really wanted to kill her cousin now. "No, no... you don't want to see them. They're really ugly and—"

"I think you're just being modest," said James with a smile.

"Yeah, quit stalling," said Pomona.

Caitlyn ground her teeth. With both of them looking at her expectantly, she had no choice. Reluctantly, she put her hand out and slowly unfurled her fingers. She cringed at the thought of their faces when they saw the fangs. How was she going to explain that one? *If only the fangs could really be chocolate,* she thought fervently.

"Oh, awesome! Chocolate fangs!" cried Pomona. "Yeah, I told you the Widow Mags should sell more chocolate body parts! That's a great idea—I bet fangs will be a huge bestseller."

"Huh?" Caitlyn looked down at her hand and blinked in surprise. Two pieces of glossy dark chocolate lay in her palm, curved and smooth, each with a pointed tip: the perfect replica of a pair of fangs. She stared. Somehow, she had really turned Viktor's fangs into chocolate!

"Do they taste good too?" asked Pomona, reaching towards her hand.

"Er... I haven't perfected the taste yet," said Caitlyn, yanking her hand back and stuffing the chocolate fangs into her pocket. "Anyway, why don't we taste the Widow Mags's samples?"

To her relief, the others turned to the rest of the

chocolates in the box, and once they'd started tasting the mouth-watering truffles and bonbons, they soon forgot all about her "creations".

Caitlyn kept the fangs safely in her pocket until Pomona dropped her back at *Bewitched by Chocolate* later that night. The Widow Mags had given her a key to the back door and she tried to be as quiet as possible as she entered the darkened kitchen, but she had barely stepped into the room when she nearly tripped over something huddled on the floor.

"Ouch!" came a grouchy old voice.

"Viktor!" Caitlyn said.

She groped on the wall nearby and flipped the light switch, flooding the kitchen with light and revealing an old man in a dusty black suit, on his hands and knees, searching for something on the floor.

"What on earth are you doing?" she asked.

"Looking for my fangs, of course," said the old vampire testily. "I haven't been able to find them since yesterday. Have you seen them?"

"Yes, they were in that box of chocolate samples sent up to the Manor," said Caitlyn in exasperation.

"Ah, yes, of course—the chocolates!" He brightened and got slowly to his feet, brushing himself off. "Can I have them back please?" He held his hand out.

"Um…there's just one problem, Viktor…" Caitlyn shifted uncomfortably.

He frowned. "What problem?"

"Well, you see... I've... er... sort of turned them into chocolate."

"You've what?"

Sheepishly, Caitlyn dug in her pocket and held out her hand to show him the two lumpy oblongs of chocolate in her palm. Viktor stared at them in horror.

"Those are my fangs?"

Caitlyn squirmed slightly. "Yes... I had no choice. James—Lord Fitzroy found them in the box and I had to think quickly, so I pretended they were chocolate fangs."

"But these... these aren't chocolate fangs!" spluttered Viktor, picking one up and holding it up to the light. "They're chocolate blobs!"

Caitlyn looked in dismay at the misshapen lump. "Um... well, I guess they melted a bit in my pocket..."

"*Melted* a bit?" Viktor looked like he was going to burst a vessel. "How am I supposed to use them now?"

"Look, there must be a way to change them back. Maybe if we—"

The door between the kitchen and the hallway opened suddenly and they both jumped. Caitlyn turned to see the Widow Mags framed in the doorway.

"Caitlyn...?" She started to say, then her eyes narrowed. "*Viktor!*"

Viktor stiffened and drew himself to his full height. "Mags."

Caitlyn gaped at one, then the other. She suddenly remembered that she had seen a photograph of a younger Viktor in the Widow Mags's old photo album. But they were certainly not eyeing each other now like long-lost friends. She wondered what their relationship was.

"It has been a long time," said Viktor, very formally.

The Widow Mags inclined her head. "Over twenty years," she said in a gruff voice. For a moment, she seemed about to say something else, then she turned to Caitlyn and said, "What's all the fuss about?"

"I... er... changed Viktor's fangs into chocolate by mistake. Well, not by mistake exactly—they were in the box of chocolate samples you sent to the Manor—"

"Still losing your fangs everywhere?" said Widow Mags, shooting Viktor a sardonic look while the old vampire bristled.

"—and I had to hide them from Lord Fitzroy and the others, so I... I'm not sure what happened but I sort of wished they could become chocolate... and then... they just turned into chocolate!" Caitlyn finished. She looked at the Widow Mags hopefully. "You can turn them back, right?"

The old witch gave her a pointed look. "You don't need me. *You* can turn them back yourself."

"Me?" Caitlyn shook her head vehemently. "No, I can't. You know I can't! I haven't even been able to bring those stupid chocolate butterflies to life and I've tried so many times now."

She looked down, ashamed of her continual failure. Ever since the Widow Mags had first shown her the spell, she had tried again and again to turn the moulded chocolate shapes into real butterflies. But the most she had managed was a slight tremble of the delicate chocolate wings.

"Maybe you're wrong," she said bitterly to the Widow Mags. "Maybe I don't have this... this 'special power' you think I have."

"It is not what I think that matters—it is what *you* think," said the old witch. "If you do not possess the magic, as you claim, then how did you change Viktor's fangs into chocolate in the first place?"

Caitlyn shrugged. "Maybe that was a fluke."

"How dare you!" cried Viktor. "I'll have you know that my teeth are quite clean and do not harbour any parasitic flatworms!"

"No, I mean, it was just luck," said Caitlyn. "I really didn't know what I was doing—"

"You followed your natural instincts," said the Widow Mags. "You let your feelings guide you and not your thoughts."

The old witch walked over and plucked the chocolate blobs out of Viktor's hands, then held them out to Caitlyn, who took them reluctantly.

"Try it now," the Widow Mags commanded.

"I... I don't know the words for the spell."

"Remember, magic comes from the force of your mind, not the words themselves," the old woman said. "However, yes, when you are inexperienced, the words of a spell can help you to focus." She cleared her throat and chanted:

"In chocolate these two fangs are cast,
To be until the very last,
But with this spell, again they'll gleam
And take their form as bat dentine."

"Now, you try." She nodded towards the chocolate lumps.

Caitlyn sighed and turned away, muttering, "Here goes nothing..."

She stared at the two blobs of chocolate and repeated the words of the spell, imagining them changing back into a pair of yellow fangs. But it was hard to concentrate. She was very aware of the Widow Mags and Viktor, both watching her intently, and she gave up almost as soon as she started.

"I can't," she said, tossing the chocolate lumps onto the kitchen table in frustration. "I just knew it wouldn't work!"

"When you start something intending to fail, that is what happens," said the Widow Mags quietly.

"I didn't 'intend to fail'!" Caitlyn flared.

"You didn't believe you would succeed, which

amounts to the same thing."

The old witch walked over to the table and picked up the blobs of chocolate. Laying them on one palm, she passed her other hand over them, saying softly, "*In chocolate these two fangs are cast, to be until the very last, but with this spell, again they'll gleam and take their form as bat dentine.*"

Caitlyn watched, dumbfounded, as the chocolate blobs trembled, then stretched and curved, their surfaces smoothing and changing from dark brown to pale ivory.

"My fangs!" cried Viktor in delight, snatching up the yellowed teeth.

"You make it look so easy," said Caitlyn wistfully.

The Widow Mags straightened to her full height. "The difficulty isn't learning to do the spell. The difficulty is believing you can. Magic only works if you really believe."

CHAPTER SEVENTEEN

Caitlyn was up bright and early the next morning, and down at *Herbal Enchantments* before breakfast. Although it was Sunday, the store was already open and Bertha was busy with a couple of Japanese tourists. Giving her aunt a wave and hoping that she would remain engaged with customers, Caitlyn hurried into the back of the cottage where she found Evie slouched over the kitchen counter, desultorily having some cereal.

"Oh, hi, Caitlyn... are you looking for Pomona? She's not up yet."

"No, Evie—I wanted to speak to you."

"Oh." The younger girl looked at her warily.

Caitlyn glanced over her shoulder to make sure that they were still alone, then lowered her voice and leaned across the counter.

"Evie, you've got to tell me the truth about Mandy Harper's murder."

Evie turned pale. "Wh-what do you mean?" she stammered.

"You lied to the police—and to me. You said you were in bed on the night of Mandy's murder."

"That's... that's right." Evie's lips trembled.

"Then how can you explain that your fingerprints were found on the cupboard in the stillroom? You were there that night, weren't you? You went to steal the love potion."

Evie lost all colour in her face. "The police found my prints?" she whispered.

"Yes, but I covered for you. I told them that you helped Grandma put the potion back, which explains why your prints are on the cupboard door. But we both know that's not true. You never went near the cupboard when we were all in the kitchen together. So the only way your prints could have been on it was if you returned later that night. I'm right, aren't I?"

Evie hesitated, then nodded miserably. "Y-yes... I went back."

"And you stole the 'love-in-idleness' extract?"

"No, not the whole thing! I only took a bit—I poured some into my own bottle. And then I heard a noise... I thought it was... I panicked and ran out..." Evie gave her a wild-eyed look. "But I swear, I didn't see Mandy! I didn't kill her! I just—"

Caitlyn put a steadying hand on the other girl's

arm and spoke soothingly: "Okay, calm down, calm down. Tell me what happened. From the beginning."

Evie took a shuddering breath. "I couldn't stop thinking about the love potion after Mum and I went home... I just... I kept thinking how easy it would be... and no one would know... and then maybe he would—" She broke off, blushing, and looked away. "Anyway, I couldn't sleep, I just kept thinking about it... and then... I thought, why not? So I got dressed and went to Grandma's cottage. I know the shortcut through the forest around the back of the houses, and I know where Grandma keeps her spare key for the back door. Anyway, even if I couldn't get the key, I knew I could simply use the Unlocking Spell—"

"*Aperio*," said Caitlyn suddenly.

Evie looked at her curiously. "Yes, that's right. It's also what opens the cupboard in the stillroom. There are too many dangerous ingredients in that cupboard, you see, so Grandma doesn't like to rely on a normal lock. Since it's locked magically, only a witch can open it."

"But if that's the case, how did Mandy manage to open it?"

Evie hung her head. "I think that was my fault. As I was pouring some of the love potion into my bottle, I heard a noise and I panicked. I thought maybe it was Grandma waking up—I knew she'd be furious if she found out that I was stealing some of the love potion. So I just shoved the vial back on the shelf and ran out of the cottage as fast as I could. I didn't stop until I got back here. I suppose I didn't close the cupboard door properly, or the back door either."

"Did you see anyone when you ran out of the cottage?"

"No, although I wasn't really looking. I just wanted to get away as quickly as possible. Why? Do you think somebody was out there?"

Caitlyn nodded. "I think Mandy Harper was watching you."

Evie stared at her. "*Mandy?*"

"Yes, I think she followed you from your place and watched while you were in the kitchen."

"But... why would you think Mandy would follow me?"

"Because I was speaking to Chris Bottom yesterday evening and he mentioned you—"

"Chris mentioned *me*?" Evie's voice went up several octaves.

"Yes, it was when I asked him about Mandy—he said she told him she planned to go to your place late that night."

"Chris mentioned me...?" asked Evie again faintly.

"Evie, are you listening? I think Mandy was planning to play a mean trick on you. She came over here and happened to see you creep out—so she decided to follow you instead. She probably followed you all the way to Grandma's cottage and watched you pour some liquid from the vial in the stillroom cupboard. Then, after you ran off, she must have decided to see what you were stealing."

"I thought he didn't even know I existed..."

Caitlyn rolled her eyes. "Evie, this is important—I'm trying to work out what happened that night! Listen, have you done *A Midsummer Night's Dream* at school?"

"*A Midsummer Night's Dream*?" Evie looked at her blankly.

"Yes, Shakespeare's play. Have you done it in class?"

Slowly, Evie nodded. "Yeah, we did it in English last year."

"Well, then Mandy could have recognised the name—'love-in-idleness'—on the tag." In her mind's eye, Caitlyn could see the dead girl's smirk as she stared down at the label and put two and two together. How gleeful she must have felt at the thought of making fun of Evie stealing a "love potion".

"The thing I can't work out is what happened after that—did she decide to steal the potion herself?" Caitlyn mused. "Or maybe she was startled by a noise too and panicked and ran out, still clutching the potion? Yes, I think that's probably what happened, because the cupboard door and the back door were both left open, as if someone had rushed out in a hurry. So if Mandy rushed out... and bumped into someone just as she was running out of the cottage... and the police say there were signs of a struggle..."

Mention of the police finally broke through Evie's daze. She looked up and said frantically, "It wasn't me! I never saw Mandy! I just rushed out and ran back here as fast as I could. You've got to believe me!"

"I do believe you, and I'm sure the police will believe you too if you tell them—"

"No!" cried Evie, taking a step backwards. "I'm not going to the police!"

"Evie, they need to know what happened—"

Evie shook her head violently. "No, if I tell them I was there that night, they'll think I'm the murderer! Everyone in the village is already talking about me. I saw some of my classmates down by the village green yesterday and they looked at me funny. They think I put a hex on Mandy."

"Well, that's just them being silly," said Caitlyn impatiently. "But the police are different. You know Inspector Walsh doesn't believe in magic—"

"Yes, but he still thinks I'm a suspect! He was here yesterday asking all sorts of questions about Mandy and whether we got on with each other and stuff... I know he's spoken to some of my teachers and other students at school, to ask if anyone has seen us fighting." She looked at Caitlyn pleadingly. "He'd never believe me if I told him that I stole the potion but didn't see Mandy that night."

Caitlyn shifted uncomfortably. Much as she

hated to admit it, she thought Evie was right. She remembered the way Inspector Walsh had looked yesterday when he had spoken of Evie. Her cousin was his top choice for a suspect at the moment and he'd be only too keen to jump on any suggestion of her guilt.

"Besides, if I tell him now, then I'd have to admit that I was lying before when I told him I was in bed, fast asleep, at the time of the murder. And he'd know that you were lying too," Evie pointed out. "He'd know that you were covering for me."

She was right. Again. Caitlyn felt torn. But before she could say anything else, there was a footstep on the kitchen threshold and both girls jerked around to see Pomona wandering into the kitchen, yawning widely.

"What's up?" she said, giving them a sleepy grin.

Evie threw Caitlyn an imploring look.

Caitlyn hesitated, then said lightly, "I... um... came to ask if you wanted to go for a drive with me? I want to go into one of the nearby towns and pick up a cat carrier."

Pomona yawned again. "Do you mind if I don't? I was just gonna have a lazy morning here, wash my hair, maybe do my nails again..." She held her bare feet out and examined her pink toenails.

"Sure, no problem. I'll see you later then." Caitlyn rose and hesitated, glancing back at Evie, but the younger girl refused to meet her eyes and, with a sigh, she turned and left the room.

CHAPTER EIGHTEEN

Caitlyn came out of *Herbal Enchantments* and walked slowly back towards the village green. She *did* believe Evie—but she had to admit that even to her own ears, the story sounded lame: to admit that you had been at the crime scene at the time of the murder and had gone to steal the very item that the murder victim had been holding... but to insist that you had nothing to do with the murder? No one would believe that. Certainly not Inspector Walsh, who was already convinced that Evie had the perfect motive.

If only there were more on the other two suspects! Caitlyn exhaled in frustration, then realised that she had arrived in the village green and was walking past the pub. She paused and looked thoughtfully up at the windows of the guest rooms on the upper level. Why couldn't she speak to Dennis Kirby herself? After all, she'd had great luck talking to Professor Ruskin—she might get some good information out of Kirby too. People were more likely to let their guard down when they weren't talking to the police.

The only thing was... would he be in his room? Caitlyn glanced at her watch. It was still very early and besides—she looked around at the empty village green—Tillyhenge was a tiny place; there wasn't much to do. Most of the shops were still closed and there was no other entertainment, unless you counted long walks in the surrounding countryside. She didn't think Dennis Kirby looked like the kind of man who would be up at the crack of dawn, hiking around the hills. There was a good chance he would still be in his room.

She headed into the pub. As she had expected, the main bar area wasn't open for business yet, but the side door which led into the adjacent hallway and the stairway to the upper rooms was open to allow the lodgers easy access. She paused at the foot of the stairs, listening. She could hear Terry, the landlord, whistling cheerfully in the bar room and a tinkling sound as he polished the glassware. From farther down the hallway came the loud whine of a vacuum cleaner, and a minute later, she caught a glimpse of Traci coming out of one room and walking into another, pushing the vacuum in front of her.

Ducking out of sight, she hurried up the stairs. At the top, she found a large bucket of soapy water, with a mop inside it, propped against the wall next to two closed doors. She wondered if Traci had been halfway through cleaning the rooms, then decided to go down and vacuum instead.

Then, angry voices from behind one of the closed doors caught her attention.

Stepping closer, Caitlyn leaned against the door and pressed her ear to the wooden surface. Luckily, these rooms had been redone with modern fittings, including cheap plywood doors instead of the original thick oak doors customary in mediaeval buildings. She could hear through them clearly, and instantly recognised the thin, quavery voice of Professor Ruskin, followed by Dennis Kirby's harsher tones.

"...you bloody tosser!" the businessman snarled. "You set the police on me!"

"What... what do you mean?" the professor asked.

"That ruddy inspector was all over me yesterday, asking about the Widow Mags and her love potion. Saying that I knew where it was and all the details of the flower it's made from. You're the only person I spoke to that night, the only one who could have told the police that I talked about it."

"But I don't see why you are upset," said the professor, sounding bewildered. "I mean, it *is* a wondrous discovery and you should be proud to tell everyone about it! You are making a huge contribution to Shakespearean scholarship. Just imagine! This is the real potion made from the 'love-in-idleness' flower, the potion used by the King of the Fairies to—"

"Oh, sod your bloody fairies! Don't you get it, you gibbering fool? Now the police think I've got a motive to kill the girl! They think I'm after the potion and will do anything to get it—"

"But that's true, isn't it? You said yourself that night—"

"Shut up about what I said! God, I wish we never had those drinks together! What was I thinking, telling you about... must have had one too many... Listen, you better keep quiet from now on about our talk that night or you'll be sorry! D'you hear me?" There was a rustle from inside the room, then Dennis Kirby spoke again, his voice low and menacing. "And you might act all innocent and noble, spouting that academic scholarship claptrap, but I know you want that potion just as much as me. Yeah, don't deny it! What did you tell the police when they asked you for your alibi that night? Sleeping, were you? Well, I know for a fact that you were lying."

Professor Ruskin made a weak sound of protest but Dennis Kirby cut him off.

"Don't deny it! I saw you! I saw you from my window as I was talking on the phone. You were scurrying off into the forest, just after the barmaid went out. Yeah, that's right. You didn't think anyone else saw you, did you? And it was just before midnight—more than enough time for you to get to the chocolate shop and murder that girl."

There was a gasp. "I did not murder that poor girl! I did not go anywhere near the chocolate shop. I simply went into the forest to look for fairy rings—"

"Don't give me that rubbish! Your nutty professor routine might work with the police but it won't work on me. I'm sure the inspector would be well interested to hear that you lied about your alibi. So if you know what's good for you, keep your gob shut!"

"But I promise you, I really was—"

"Shut up! SHUT UP!"

There was a loud *whack* as if someone had slammed a hand against a table. Caitlyn jerked back reflexively and her elbow knocked against something which clattered onto the wooden landing. She turned and realised that she had bumped into the mop leaning against the wall. It had fallen out of the bucket and sloshed soapy water everywhere. Before she could react, however, she heard footsteps approaching and the door was yanked open.

"What the—!" Dennis Kirby stood glaring in the doorway, with Professor Ruskin hovering behind him.

Caitlyn froze on the landing, staring at him like

the proverbial rabbit caught in the headlights. He stared back at her for a moment, an ugly expression on his face, then with a muttered curse, he pushed roughly past her and stormed down the stairs. A second later, the side door of the pub slammed.

Caitlyn let out the breath she didn't know she had been holding. Even though she knew that it was broad daylight in a public place, there was something about Kirby that put you on edge. He was the kind of man who would probably lose his temper and punch you in the face, even in a crowded room. She glanced back to see Professor Ruskin standing in the doorway, clutching a book, an expression of mingled nervousness and relief on his face.

Caitlyn cleared her throat. "I... um... couldn't help overhearing just now. You know, if he's threatening you, you should go to the police—"

The professor flushed. "Right... Yes, well... I'm very busy, I'm afraid... a lot of work to do... journals, you know... academic papers... Please excuse me," he mumbled, shutting the door in her face.

Caitlyn stood staring at the closed door for a moment. Then, with a sigh, she turned and went back downstairs.

CHAPTER NINETEEN

Somehow, Caitlyn drove out of Tillyhenge and into the nearest market town, although she was hardly aware of doing it. Her mind was buzzing with what she had just overheard in the pub and she couldn't stop herself mulling over the mystery of Mandy Harper's murder.

So Professor Ruskin had lied to the police about his alibi? Why? She couldn't help wondering if Dennis Kirby was right and the "nutty professor" persona really was just an act put on for the benefit of the police. After all, it would be a clever strategy—it gave Ruskin the perfect excuse to have an interest in the potion and to skulk about in the forest without anyone getting suspicious. And with his constant talk of fairies and Shakespeare, no one took him seriously. Most people thought him to be a harmless, crazy old man... which was a perfect disguise for a murderer.

Still, Caitlyn found it hard to wrap her head around the thought of Professor Ruskin as a killer. Not when there were much more likely candidates, like Dennis Kirby, around. Her encounter with the businessman this morning seemed to confirm even more that he had a foul temper and was likely to get physically abusive when angry. She could just see him struggling with Mandy, demanding that the girl give him the potion, and then getting violent when she refused. And it certainly fit with him being furious at the professor for telling the police about his knowledge of the potion. If he really had killed Mandy and stolen it, he would obviously want to lie low until the police were obliged to remove him from their investigation and he could leave Tillyhenge with the precious potion secretly in his possession.

Caitlyn parked in the large supermarket car park and wandered down the pedestrianised main street nearby, still in a preoccupied daze. It was strange being back in a busy town again, surrounded by crowds of people and the flashing lights and incessant hum of traffic and modern technology. She blinked as she walked past several fast food outlets, their neon signs garish in the morning light, and stared bemusedly at the window of a mobile phone store, where a giant interactive video display announced the arrival of the latest iPhone. It felt almost as if she had been away in another world and had just returned to join the twenty-first century.

She located the pet store and was pleased to find a light wicker cat carrier which would be perfect for Nibs. As she stepped out of the store, Caitlyn's stomach rumbled and she remembered belatedly that she hadn't had any breakfast yet. She glanced across the street. There was a café opposite the pet store, with a large A-frame sign on the pavement outside showing a mouth-watering picture and a line advertising the daily special of "*Heavenly hot chocolate with whipped cream and chocolate sprinkles!*"

Mmm... Caitlyn had a sudden craving for the Widow Mags's delicious rich hot chocolate. This wasn't the same, of course, but from the look of the picture, it wouldn't be a bad substitute. She hurried into the café and ordered with eager anticipation. But when the waitress finally brought the order to her table, Caitlyn stared at it in disappointment. It looked nothing like the advert! The cheap ceramic mug was filled with a murky brown liquid, with a blob of what looked like shaving foam floating forlornly in the centre. Chocolate powder had been scattered carelessly over the drink, ending up mostly on the rim and down the outside of the cup.

Picking up the mug gingerly, Caitlyn took a cautious sip, then recoiled, making a face. She stared at the murky brown liquid in disbelief. She couldn't believe they had the gall to call this "chocolate"! It was sweet and sickly, with a weak artificial flavour and watery consistency. Even hungry as she was, she couldn't bring herself to drink more of it.

Instead, she turned her attention to the piece of chocolate cake that she had ordered as well and eyed it warily. It was a thin wedge of limp brown sponge with a layer of dried crusty frosting on top. It, too, looked nothing like the advert outside, but her stomach was rumbling so Caitlyn picked up her fork and cut off a small section. She put it tentatively in her mouth. It wasn't quite as disgusting as the hot chocolate (which wasn't saying much) but it was soggy and tasteless, like chewing wet newspaper.

Caitlyn sighed and pushed the plate away. Her stomach growled again in protest and she turned to look at the wall menu, wondering if she dared try anything else. Then she noticed two people who had just entered the café: a lanky teenage boy with a mop of sun-streaked blond hair and a tall, dark-haired man with handsome, aristocratic features. Chris Bottom and James Fitzroy.

Caitlyn felt the familiar shyness and self-consciousness overcome her. Despite being casually dressed in dark jeans and an open-necked shirt, James looked suave and sexy, with the fine cotton fabric of his shirt stretched across his broad shoulders and his tanned muscular forearms displayed by the rolled-up sleeves. She wished suddenly that she had taken more pains with her appearance that morning. At least she wasn't wearing her usual old faded jeans, but she wasn't sure her choice of cotton camisole and loose linen skirt was much better. Did the pleats on the skirt make her hips look even bigger? And didn't linen wrinkle horribly? She shuddered to think what her behind must look like if she stood up now from her seat.

Maybe they won't notice me, she thought, shrinking down in her chair. But the next moment, James turned from looking at the wall menu and caught sight of her. His grey eyes lit up and he came swiftly across the room.

"Caitlyn! This is a pleasant surprise." His gaze shifted downwards to her table and he groaned in dismay. "Don't tell me you've ordered the chocolate special. That thing should come with a public health warning!"

Caitlyn laughed, her shyness evaporating at their shared disgust over the chocolate. "Yes. I got sucked in by the advertising outside. I came into town to buy a cat carrier but I missed breakfast this morning and I was starving, so when I saw the poster... Well, I'm regretting it now."

"Hang on—don't move. I'll be right back," said James.

He hurried to where Chris was still waiting at the counter and returned a few minutes later with the boy, both of them carrying trays laden with drinks and food.

"Here you go," said James, unloading the items on the table.

Caitlyn watched in bemusement as he set out a large pot of tea and three cups, a plate of Chelsea buns, another of toasted oatcakes, several muffins, and a pot of jam, followed by a small dish of fresh butter.

"Not quite a proper full English breakfast but it'll probably do the trick," said James with a chuckle as he sat down at the table next to her.

Chris sat down as well, then jumped up again, sneezing violently. "Sorry," he mumbled. "Hay fever."

Caitlyn handed him a napkin, feeling sorry for the boy. He looked like he was really suffering, with his nose red and his eyes watery and swollen.

James picked up the plate of warm oatcakes and held it out towards her. "Go on. Help yourself."

Not wanting to appear rude, Caitlyn took one, but she braced herself as she bit into the round, biscuit-like bread. To her surprise, it was actually very good, with a strong oaty flavour, a chewy texture, and a hint of saltiness, which was offset by the slather of butter and home-made jam.

"This is very nice," she said in surprise.

"Yes, most of the food here is pretty good. I learned the hard way to avoid the chocolate items," said James with a rueful grin. "Sorry, I probably should have warned you the other day, when you were talking about coming into town."

He jerked his head towards the menu on the wall. Caitlyn followed the direction of his gaze and realised that there was a small logo stamped in the corner of the menu, with the words "Sponsored by Kirby Chocolates" printed underneath.

"Kirby's stuff is shi—sorry, I mean, awful," said Chris thickly.

James nodded. "Most of us locals know to avoid it and it's only the tourists who get taken in. He's good at marketing, I'll hand him that. He knows all the right things to say to make his products sound delicious."

Caitlyn thought back to that enticing advert outside and felt annoyed. She *had* been completely fooled by the slick marketing. Then she thought of the Widow Mags's rich, mouth-watering, hand-made chocolates and felt a pang of sadness at the thought of people paying to eat this rubbish when there was something so much better only a few miles away.

Then she thought of something else. She hesitated, looking sideways at James, then took a breath and said, "Um… speaking of Dennis Kirby, I heard something interesting this morning. Something which could have some bearing on Mandy Harper's murder."

James's gaze sharpened. "Yes?"

Caitlyn recounted the scene she had overheard at the pub.

When she finished, Chris whistled and said, "He sounds a right dodgy bloke, that Kirby. Like the type that could murder anyone."

James frowned. "He's certainly obnoxious, but I'm not sure that means that he's guilty."

Caitlyn protested, "But... but he was so worried about Professor Ruskin telling the police that he knew about the love potion—"

"Yes, but that *could* just be general annoyance. No one likes to be tied to a murder inquiry. He could simply have been angry that Ruskin was making the police suspect him."

"He *was* the person eavesdropping outside the kitchen!" Caitlyn insisted. "Which means he heard the Widow Mags talk about the potion and knew where it was kept."

"Yes, but that doesn't necessarily mean that he was the one who murdered Mandy," James pointed out. "He could have bragged to Ruskin about the potion, yes, and talked about what he would do when he got his hands on it—but that could be just that: talk. It doesn't mean he went out that night to break into the Widow Mags's cottage. In any case, it's just too much of a coincidence that he should steal the potion and Mandy should happen to be there too—how would she have known that he was going to steal it? She had no connection with him."

"It wasn't Kirby who stole the love potion from the stillroom," said Caitlyn impatiently. "He probably came after Mandy got hold of it."

James frowned. "But then how did Mandy know where the potion was? She wasn't the one eavesdropping outside the kitchen window."

"Because she followed—" Caitlyn broke off suddenly, realising what she had almost blurted out.

"Yes?"

"N-nothing," stammered Caitlyn. "Um... Anyway, the point is, the police should search Kirby's belongings. Just in case."

"They'll need to get a search warrant, I think, especially without more specific proof to tie him to the murder," said James.

"Well, they can do that, can't they?"

"Yes, of course, but I don't know how keen Inspector Walsh would be to make the effort. To be honest with you, he's not particularly enthusiastic about that line of enquiry. He can't believe that someone would really kill for a so-called 'love potion'... and in any case, Kirby has an alibi," James reminded her. "That's the most important thing where the police are concerned. A man can't be arrested for murder if there is proof that he was elsewhere at the time of the crime."

CHAPTER TWENTY

There was no more talk of the murder as they finished breakfast. Instead, the conversation turned back to Ferdinand the bull.

"Dad is getting really frustrated," said Chris. "He says the vet found nothing wrong with Ferdinand and all the tests came back normal."

"I don't understand it either," said James, shaking his head. "If this bovine expert doesn't have any solutions for us on Monday, I think I might have to take Pomona's suggestion and find a cow whisperer!"

Caitlyn stifled a giggle. "The scary thing is, such a thing probably exists in Hollywood… Oh, no thanks," she said as James offered her another muffin. "Can I have one of the Chelsea buns instead? I love Chelsea buns and these are really good, with just the right balance of cinnamon and lemon zest, and raisins scattered evenly through the dough."

James gave her a curious look as he passed her the plate of sweet, sticky rolls. "You seem to know a lot about British baking. Most Americans would just call them cinnamon rolls."

Caitlyn smiled self-consciously. "Well, you know I didn't really grow up in the U.S., despite Barbara being American... so I guess I'm not a typical 'American'."

"Barbara?" said Chris, looking puzzled.

"Barbara Le Fey," James explained. "She was Caitlyn's mother."

"What... you mean Barbara Le Fey, the singer?" Chris turned to Caitlyn, his eyes wide. "Your mother's the famous—"

"Barbara was my adoptive mother," Caitlyn said quickly. "I was actually born here, in the Cotswolds, and she adopted me when I was a baby. But I didn't see much of her growing up—I guess it's the same for a lot of kids with celebrity parents. I had a British nanny and she was the one who really brought me up." She smiled in reminiscence. "She taught me all about traditional British baking and desserts—like scones and treacle tarts and sticky toffee pudding... She loved to bake so I got to taste home-made versions of all the things she talked about."

"Sounds like you had a very British upbringing

in many respects," said James.

"Yes." Caitlyn gave him a shy look. "I was home-schooled too. My nanny stayed on as a sort of home-tutor-slash-governess as I got older. So combined with the fact that we were always travelling overseas and never really lived in the States—well, in a way, I feel more English than American."

"You sound it too," said James with a laugh. "I noticed your unusual accent the first time I met you."

Caitlyn gave another self-conscious smile. "Yes, I suppose I talk a bit 'funny'..."

"'Funny' isn't the word I would have used," James said, his grey eyes twinkling. "I think it's a charming accent."

Caitlyn blushed and looked away. She was almost glad when Chris began sneezing again, diverting the attention. She watched him sympathetically as he doubled over, sneezing three times in a row, then groped blearily for another napkin to blow his nose.

"You should go get some hay fever pills from the chemist," said James in concern.

Chris shook his head miserably, mopping his nose. "Don't like those—make me drowsy," he mumbled.

"Have you tried any herbal remedies?" asked Caitlyn.

"Herbal remedies?"

Caitlyn nodded. "I was in *Herbal Enchantments* yesterday—you know, Evie's mother's store—and a couple of tourists came in asking about a hay fever tonic. I heard one of them saying how effective it was—even better than the stuff they got from the pharmacy. Maybe you could give that a try?"

Chris gave her a shifty look. "Uh... Not sure... I mean, my Aunt Vera—that's Dad's older sister—told me never to get anything from that shop..."

"Why ever not?" asked James in surprise.

Chris looked embarrassed. "There's talk in the village about Evie's mother... you know, that she's a witch, like the Widow Mags... and Aunt Vera says—"

James roared with laughter. "Bertha's not a witch! She is just a very competent herbalist. And you can tell your aunt that she's actually a consultant and supplier to one of the largest commercial manufacturers of herbal remedies in the U.K. Her preparations are sold in stores all over England." He put a hand on Chris's shoulder. "So tell your aunt to stop worrying. If the biggest herbal company in the U.K. can trust Bertha, I'm sure you can."

Of course, it makes perfect sense, Caitlyn thought. She'd always wondered why Bertha wasn't as much of an outcast and how her aunt managed to have a healthy income—and support the Widow Mags too—given that *Herbal Enchantments* seemed to be empty a lot of the time.

"Caitlyn, are you heading back to the village now?" asked James.

She nodded.

"Do you mind taking Chris back to Tillyhenge with you? I've still got to pick up a few things from the shops but there's no need for him to—"

"I'm all right," protested Chris. "I'm fine, honestly. I just—ah—ahh—AHH—ATCHOO!"

James gave him a grin. "No need for heroics, Chris. Go on—go with Caitlyn. You'll do more good sorting yourself out than sneezing all over me."

***

"He's a top guy, James—I mean, Lord Fitzroy—isn't he?" said Chris enthusiastically as they left the car parked in the village green and began walking towards *Herbal Enchantments.*

Caitlyn smiled. It wasn't the first time she'd heard the villagers praise James. When she first arrived in Tillyhenge, she had been a bit shocked to discover that it was one of the last pockets in England where the old-fashioned "feudal" system still survived. But while James really was "lord of the manor", owning all the surrounding farms and estates, as well as the village itself, he was nothing like the evil squire stereotype often found in historical novels. His tenants all seemed to adore him and Caitlyn had never heard anyone say a bad word about him.

"Yes, he's wonderful!" she agreed. "I've only been in Tillyhenge a short while but I can already see what a generous and responsible landlord he is. And it's not just that—he's got such a nice manner. He treats everybody the same and never throws his title around. You just instantly like him and respect him." Realising belatedly that her effusive praise might be misinterpreted, she blushed and added, "Of course, I'm sure his father, the old Lord Fitzroy, was the same."

"Don't you believe it," said Chris with a dark look. "I mean, he was a good landlord too and all that—my Dad says the Fitzroys have always been decent and done right by their tenants—but old Lord Fitzroy was a bit of a pompous git. He'd never roll his sleeves up and muck in down on the farms, like James does, or talk to you like a friend. You know, when he died last year, my Dad was worried about his son coming back to take over." He grinned. "Now he thinks it's the best thing that's happened to Tillyhenge."

They arrived at the herbal store and found it empty except for Evie, who was standing behind the counter, carefully portioning pale yellow powder into individual paper sachets, her tongue stuck between her teeth in concentration.

"Hi Evie," Caitlyn called as they entered.

The teenage girl looked up, then did a double take as she saw Chris. Her hands jerked and powder spilled everywhere.

"H-h-hi..." she stammered, flushing bright red.

"Evie, is your mum around? Chris is really suffering and I heard a customer yesterday say one of your mother's tonics worked fantastic for her hay fever."

Evie shook her head. "She's gone into town..."

"Well, do you know where your mother keeps her hay fever remedies?"

Evie nodded, her eyes still glued on Chris, who gave her a wan smile before sneezing violently again.

"I'll... I'll just go and get some..." Evie whispered.

She turned and dashed into the back of the building. She was gone a long time and there seemed to be a lot of strange noises coming from the back, as well as the faint smell of burning candles. Caitlyn was just beginning to wonder if she should go check for herself when Evie re-emerged, very flushed, with her hair slightly wild and her eyes overly bright. She was holding a bowl with two hands, carrying it with great care.

"Er... is that the tonic?" asked Caitlyn, eyeing the bowl uncertainly. The dark liquid seemed to be smoking slightly.

"Yes," said Evie breathlessly. She approached Chris and held it out to him with shaking hands. "H-here you go. You need to drink it all up."

Chris took the concoction with a doubtful look, but dutifully raised the bowl to his lips and began drinking. Caitlyn watched his Adam's apple bobbing up and down as he finished the entire bowl, then put it down on the counter, grimacing slightly. Evie hovered in front of him, her eyes enormous as she stared up into his face.

"H-how do you feel?" she asked Chris.

He made a face. "Dunno..."

"Is your nose less stuffy?" asked Caitlyn. "Do your eyes feel less itchy?"

"I dunno..." said Chris again. "I... I feel a bit weird..."

He shook his head and Caitlyn couldn't help noticing that his ears looked slightly strange. She blinked and looked again. Was she dreaming or did his ears seem a bit... elongated? She shook her own head. She must have been imagining things. But the next moment, she stared in shock. No, she wasn't imagining things: Chris's ears were elongating before her very eyes, changing from round shells of smooth pink cartilage into long pointed lobes covered in grey fur...

Donkey ears!

There was a loud gasp from Evie. She was still staring at Chris but, instead of hopeful anticipation, there was now incredulous horror in the girl's eyes. She had both hands clamped over her mouth and was making inarticulate sounds.

"Evie—what's happening?" asked Caitlyn in an urgent whisper.

"I... I..." Evie looked sick. "I don't know... It should have worked!"

"Are you sure you got the right tonic?" asked Caitlyn. "Maybe this is a remedy for something else?"

Although she couldn't, for the life of her, think what anyone would want to drink this tonic for. Not only did Chris now have giant donkey ears sprouting out of his head, but his face was also changing, his nose enlarging and stretching downwards, and his hair morphing into a thatch of thick dark-grey fur on his forehead. He held out his bare arms, which were also becoming covered in a coat of pale grey fur, and looked down at them in bewilderment.

"What's happening to me?" he said, his voice thick and strange. "I feel really fun*ee…hee…hee-haw…HEE-HAW!"*

Caitlyn watched in stupefied horror as Chris's face disappeared completely, his nose elongating into a snout with a velvety muzzle, his neck stretching into a furry crest, and his body hunching forwards onto all fours, with a rounded rump, sturdy legs, and soft, fuzzy grey fur all over… until finally, in place of the teenage boy, there was a furry little donkey, with wide brown eyes, looking up at them.

CHAPTER TWENTY-ONE

"Oh my God, Evie, what have you done?" Caitlyn cried. "What did you give him?"

Evie gave a frightened whimper. "It's... it's all wrong. It shouldn't happen like this... He's supposed to... to... look at me and then—"

"*What did you give him?*" Caitlyn demanded.

"I... I gave him some of Mum's hay fever tonic... mixed with some... um... some..." Evie blushed furiously and couldn't meet her eyes. "...Some love potion," she finally said, so low that Caitlyn almost couldn't hear her.

"Love potion? You mean the 'love-in-idleness' extract?"

"I told you—I poured some from Grandma's vial into my own bottle that night when I sneaked into the stillroom. I thought maybe if Chris... you know... I mean, it wouldn't hurt him. It would just make him... well..." Evie's voice sank to a whisper. "...you know... *like* me more."

Caitlyn stared at the younger girl, torn between exasperation and compassion. Then she glanced at the donkey, which was now sniffing the nearby shelf of natural loofah sponges with great interest.

"But... I don't understand..." she said. "A love potion is supposed to make people fall in love—not turn people into donkeys!"

"Well, um... I sort of tweaked it a bit..." said Evie, shifting uncomfortably. "I mean, you can't just use the extract by itself—you need a spell as well."

Suddenly, Caitlyn remembered the Widow Mags's words:

"Love magic is a complicated thing. Certainly, a potion can be created to evoke the feelings of yearning and desire, of tenderness and contentment, but a spell is also required to direct those feelings towards the right person. And that can be tricky—very tricky..."

Evie's track record of using spells and magic was pretty shaky at the best of times. The girl had trouble even doing simple things, like enchanting brooms to sweep a room. Caitlyn shuddered to think what her cousin might have done with something as complicated as love magic.

"I followed the instructions for the spell exactly!" Evie insisted. "I found it in this old book that Mum keeps in her bedroom. It's called *Ancient Love*

Magick for Revealing the Face of True Love."

"Well, you must have done something wrong," said Caitlyn dryly. "Unless the Face of True Love is a horsey, furry one." She glanced at the donkey again, then cried, "Hey! Stop! Don't eat that!"

"*HEE-HAW!*" brayed the donkey, ignoring her and continuing to chew the loofah sponge.

"Oh no!" cried Evie, running forwards and trying to tug the sponge out of the donkey's mouth. "Mum just got those delivered from Egypt last week!"

Both girls grabbed the loofah and tried to pull it from the donkey. But the furry little beast was strong and it wasn't giving up its new toy any time soon. The two girls soon found themselves in a desperate tug-o-war, heaving in one direction while the donkey yanked in the other, its neck extended and its big prominent teeth clamped on the loofah.

"*HEE-HAW! HEE-HAW!*" it brayed indignantly.

"LET... GO!" Caitlyn panted, throwing her weight backwards.

"Caitlyn?"

She whirled around, her heart sinking to her feet as she saw who was standing in the shop doorway. It was James Fitzroy, looking at them in utter bewilderment.

"Uh... James!" Caitlyn gasped, letting go of the loofah.

"Aaah!" cried Evie, lurching forwards as the donkey took advantage of the loosened grip and yanked the sponge out her hands.

Caitlyn plastered a shaky smile to her face. "Um, hello, James... can we help you?"

"*HEE-HAW... HEE-HAW... HEE-HAW!*" brayed the donkey, trotting triumphantly around them, shaking the loofah sponge in his mouth.

James tore his gaze from the gambolling creature. "Er... You do realise there's a donkey loose in the store?"

"Oh yes," said Caitlyn airily, as if screeching donkeys came into the store every day.

James looked at Evie. "Where did you get him from? I don't remember any of the farms on the estate having a donkey."

"Um... he's..." Evie's expression went blank.

"He's a special import!" cried Caitlyn. "Pomona brought him from London!"

"Did I hear my name?" asked Pomona, sauntering out of the doorway at the back of the shop and strolling over to join them. She was wearing a fluffy pink bathrobe and had her hair wrapped up in a towel turban. Grinning at Evie, she said, "Omigod, that organic shampoo is awesome! I gotta get some before I leave. In fact, have you thought about exporting to the States? I know a couple of shops in L.A. that would love—*Holy guacamole! Is that a donkey?*"

"Yes, you brought him from London, *remember*?" said Caitlyn, stamping on her cousin's foot.

"*OW! What did you*—I did?" Pomona's scowl changed to a look of understanding as she met

Caitlyn's pleading eyes. "Oh yes, of course I did!"

"Why?" asked James, puzzled.

"Why? Er..." Pomona gave Caitlyn a panicked look behind James's back and made frantic *"What now?"* hand gestures. "Um... well, I had this idea for... uh... a mascot! Yeah, a shop mascot!"

James frowned. "A shop mascot?"

"Yeah, you know—like sports team mascots in the U.S.—er... all the best shops in Hollywood have them now. And donkeys are one of the hottest mascots at the moment!"

"They are?" James looked even more incredulous.

"Oh yeah, donkeys are very... uh... *zen*... animals to have around. Great for your... um... blood pressure, you know..." Pomona babbled, trying to ignore the sound of loud chewing coming from behind them. The donkey had finally lost interest in the loofah sponge and was now trying to eat the bamboo blinds at the window. Evie gasped and rushed across the room. A minute later, they heard a mixture of indignant snorting and desperate cries of "Argh! Let go! *Let go!*"

Pomona cleared her throat and said hurriedly, "So anyway, what brings you here, James? Looking for some soya candles or herbal tea?"

"No, actually, I was looking for Chris Bottom."

Evie made a strangled sound behind them. James glanced over his shoulder at her in puzzlement, then said to Caitlyn:

"Did Chris get something for his hay fever?"

Oh, yeah, he got something all right, thought Caitlyn. Aloud, she said, "Yes, he had some of Bertha's tonic."

"And did it work?" asked James with a smile.

Caitlyn glanced at the donkey, who was now enthusiastically chewing an organic hemp hair wrap while Evie struggled to untangle the cords that pulled the blinds. "Yes… er… it had a pretty strong effect."

"*HEE-HAW!*" brayed the donkey happily.

"Has Chris gone back to the Manor then?" James asked.

"Um… I'm not sure. He… he didn't say…"

"Oh, well, Tillyhenge isn't that big. I'll have a look around—I'm sure I'll catch him." With a last doubtful glance at the donkey, James smiled at them all and left.

As soon as he was out of earshot, Pomona pounced on Caitlyn and said:

"Okay, what was that all about? I never brought any donkey from London!"

Caitlyn hurried to shut the door of the store and flip the "Open" sign to "Closed". Then she staggered back to the counter—where Evie was standing, looking slightly shell-shocked—and sagged into a chair.

"Oh, Pomie…" Caitlyn gave a ragged sigh. "That's not a donkey."

"Huh?" Pomona swung around to look at the

furry creature, who was now drinking out of the bamboo water feature. "Looks like a donkey to me."

"No, I mean—it's not *really* a donkey. It's actually a boy named Chris Bottom."

"He's a boy in my class," said Evie in a small voice. "I... I gave him a potion to drink but I must have got the spell wrong."

"What did you give him a potion for?"

Evie squirmed. "It was a... a love potion."

"Like the Widow Mags's chocolate sauce?"

"No, that just gives you the nice feeling of being in love—that's why everything the sauce is poured on tastes so delicious. This is different—this is the 'love-in-idleness' extract, combined with a spell... a love magic spell... to... to make someone fall in love with you." Evie flushed, eyeing Pomona sideways and bracing herself to be laughed at.

But Pomona looked at her with genuine interest. "What—you mean a real, honest-to-goodness love potion? So if someone drinks it, they fall in love with you? That is *so cool!* How does it work? Do you have some left? Because I would—"

"Pomona!" Caitlyn said.

"Aww, c'mon, Caitlyn! You have to admit that is freaking cool! To be able to make someone fall in love with you... I mean, not that I've ever needed—"

"But it didn't make him fall in love—it turned him into a donkey!" Caitlyn wailed.

"Oh. Yeah. There's that." Pomona sobered. "Well, what are we going to do?"

"We've got to tell the Widow Mags," said Caitlyn. "She'll know what to do—"

"NO!" cried Evie. "No, you can't tell Grandma! She'll be livid if she knew that I stole some of her potion!"

"Evie, we have no choice—we can't leave Chris like this."

"No! No, you can't tell her!"

"Maybe we can figure out how to change him back ourselves," Pomona suggested. "I mean, you just need to find the right spell for it, right?" She turned to Evie. "Where did you get the love magic spell?"

Evie hurried into the back of the cottage and returned a few minutes later carrying a thick leather-bound book with yellowed pages.

"Ooh—is that like a *grimoire*?" said Pomona, her eyes lighting up.

"No, not really. I mean, it's not Mum's *grimoire*—it's just an old book of spells that she keeps in her bedroom."

"What's a *grimoire*?" asked Caitlyn.

"It's, like, a witch's personal book of spells," said Pomona absently, taking the book and opening it with eager fingers.

As Caitlyn watched Pomona flip through the pages, she thought once again that it should really have been her cousin—and not her—who discovered that she came from a family of witches. Pomona had always been obsessed with magic and the paranormal. She knew all the folklore and rituals associated with witchcraft—or at least the popular myths and beliefs—and she embraced them whole-heartedly. Caitlyn knew that if she could just have Pomona's blind faith, magic would come to her so much more easily. She thought once again of her failure the night before with the chocolate fangs.

"Magic only works if you really believe," the Widow Mags had said.

Caitlyn knew in her heart that her grandmother was right. There was always a doubting, sceptical voice in her head whenever she tried to work magic. She had learned to ignore it sometimes but it was always there, jeering at her, telling her that it wasn't going to work, that she was going to fail. The few times when she forgot herself—such as when she was angry or terrified—magic had come to her with little effort. She thought of the way the locked doors had opened at her command when she had been desperate to rescue Nibs. She had never even practised the *Aperio* spell—and yet it had felt as familiar as if she had done it a hundred times.

Caitlyn came out of her reverie to see Pomona and Evie poring over the old book. Both looked very disheartened.

"Any luck?" Caitlyn asked.

"No, nothing," said Pomona, sitting back and heaving a sigh of frustration. "There are spells for 'Summoning a Flatter Stomach' and 'Self-Filling Money Jars' and 'Growing Wings in Two Days'... but nothing about undoing a transmutation spell!"

"Maybe we need to look in other books?" suggested Caitlyn. "Maybe—"

"I know!" cried Pomona, snapping her fingers. "I know how to undo it!"

"How?" asked both Caitlyn and Evie at once.

Pomona gave a triumphant smile. "True Love's First Kiss!"

"What?" Caitlyn gaped at her. "What are you talking about?"

"It's in all the fairy tales!" said Pomona. "Like 'Beauty and the Beast'… and 'The Frog Prince'… when someone is bewitched, the only way to break the spell is for them to be kissed by their one true love."

"But… those are just made up stories in books," protested Caitlyn. "They're not real!"

"Neither are witches," said Pomona with a look.

"Yes, but that's… different. This is… well, it's the dumbest thing I've ever heard!"

"You got a better idea?"

Caitlyn opened her mouth and shut it again. Pomona turned and looked at Evie expectantly.

The girl went bright red. "W-why are you looking at me? I don't… I'm not…"

"Oh, *pu-lease*," said Pomona, rolling her eyes. "Why did you give him a love potion then?"

"Well, I…" Evie faltered.

"C'mon! It's the only way to save him." Pomona ran across the room to the donkey, who seemed to have gone to sleep standing up, and gave it a pat to wake it up. It shook its head, making its long ears flap about, and gave a loud snort, but it followed her willingly enough when she cajoled it over to join them.

"You... you want me to kiss the donkey?" said Evie, looking slightly queasy.

"Why not? He's rather cute," Pomona chuckled, rubbing the donkey's furry ears.

"HEE-HAW!" brayed the donkey, swishing his tufted tail.

Evie swallowed and leaned slowly forwards. Then she jerked back. "What if... what if he turns back into Chris while we're still kissing?" she whispered, her face flaming.

"Well, then you'll enjoy the kiss a lot more, won't you?" said Pomona, grinning. "C'mon! Pucker up! A proper kiss now... on the lips."

Evie looked at Caitlyn, who shrugged. The teenage girl hesitated, then took a deep breath and bent down towards the donkey. It raised its head inquisitively and pulled back its whiskered lips, showing a row of big yellow teeth. Evie screwed up her face, leaned closer, and pecked the donkey's muzzle, then jerked back, staring apprehensively.

They all waited.

Nothing happened.

"Do you think it should have worked by now?" asked Evie at last.

"Hmm..." Pomona scratched her head. "Try it

again."

Evie tried again. And again. But the donkey didn't so much as change a whisker.

"I don't understand... it *should* work..." muttered Pomona. "Maybe you need to do it under moonlight? Or maybe we need to put the donkey to sleep first? I don't suppose you have any herbal sleeping tonics that're safe to give to donkeys—"

"It's because you didn't really mean it, Evie," Caitlyn spoke up. "That's why it didn't work."

Pomona and Evie looked at her blankly.

"When you kissed it—him—just now," Caitlyn explained. "You didn't really want to. You were just thinking of it as a disgusting thing you had to do. But only a True Love's First Kiss can really break the spell, right? So you have to mean it. You have to believe that you're really kissing someone you love." She paused, the Widow Mags's words coming back to her again, and she said them out loud: "Magic only works if you really believe."

Evie stared at her, then turned back to look at the donkey. Taking a deep breath, she reached out and caught the furry head between her hands. Slowly, she lowered her head and closed her eyes...

Caitlyn held her breath. Evie pressed her lips to the donkey's velvety muzzle, not jerking back this time but kissing it gently, tenderly. The little donkey made a soft sighing sound and its long eyelashes fluttered shut. Then Pomona gasped as the donkey's form quivered, seeming to shift and coalesce, like colours in a kaleidoscope, until the next moment, a lanky teenage boy stood in its place.

Chris Bottom blinked and opened his eyes, to stare straight into Evie's wide brown ones. She squeaked and jumped back, putting several feet between them.

"Chris?" Caitlyn stepped forwards and put a gentle hand on the boy's shoulder. "Are you all right?"

"Yeah..." He rubbed his eyes and looked around in bemusement. "I... think so... Have I been asleep? I had a really weird dream..."

CHAPTER TWENTY-TWO

After the morning of magical mayhem, Caitlyn hoped the rest of the day would pass uneventfully, but Chris had barely left *Herbal Enchantments*—still in a daze—when Bertha returned, accompanied by Inspector Walsh.

"Hi Bertha..." Caitlyn trailed off as she saw her aunt's pale, anxious face. "What's the matter?"

Before she could answer, Inspector Walsh marched up to Evie and said, "You've been lying to the police, young lady."

"Wh-what do you mean?" squeaked Evie.

"You told me that you were in bed the night of Mandy Harper's murder. And yet your prints were found on the stillroom cupboard. Miss Le Fey here—" he shot Caitlyn a scathing look, "—told me that you had helped your grandmother return the vial to the stillroom—that *that* was the reason your prints were all over the cupboard door... but that's not true, is it? She was covering for you, wasn't she? I have just been speaking to the Widow Mags again and she tells me that *she* was the one who replaced the vial that night. You didn't go anywhere near that cupboard. So how do you explain why your prints are on the cupboard door as well?"

"I..." Evie's eyes darted around desperately. "Well, I..."

"It's all right, dear—I'm sure there's been a misunderstanding," Bertha said, putting a hand on her daughter's arm.

"You were there that night, weren't you?" demanded Inspector Walsh. "I spoke to Chris Bottom again early this morning and he told me something very interesting: Mandy Harper had planned to sneak out and go to your place, the night she was killed. Had you arranged to meet her? Maybe you lured her out on purpose... maybe you went to the chocolate shop together and then had an argument. After all, Mandy had tormented you and bullied you regularly at school... and during the struggle, you killed her."

Bertha gasped. "Inspector! My Evie would never murder anyone!"

"I didn't!" cried Evie. "I never even saw Mandy that night!"

"Ah—so you admit that you were there?" Inspector Walsh pounced on her.

Evie hesitated, then nodded miserably. "Yes, I... I did go back to Grandma's cottage that night." She ducked her head, avoiding her mother's eyes. "I wanted to steal some of the... the love potion."

"*What?*" Bertha turned to look at her daughter, appalled.

"But that's all I did!" Evie insisted. "I never saw Mandy! I swear!"

Inspector Walsh put a hand under her elbow. "Young lady, I am taking you into custody."

"Wait—you're not arresting her?" cried Caitlyn, aghast.

"Yes, I am—and be thankful that I'm not arresting you as well, for attempting to pervert the course of justice," snapped Inspector Walsh. "You lied to me as well."

Caitlyn swallowed and watched helplessly as the inspector led Evie out of the store, with Bertha hurriedly following.

"He can't just do that!" Pomona fumed. "She needs a good lawyer. If Bertha doesn't have anyone, I can call my contacts in Hollywood—"

"I think she knows someone. When the Widow Mags was nearly arrested, I remember her mentioning a lady who specialises in defending those with 'alternative lifestyles'. I'm sure Berth will call her." Caitlyn sighed. "Oh, but Pomie... I hate to admit it, but Evie's story does sound very lame: she was there on the night of the murder, she admits to stealing the thing that the victim was holding, but insists that she didn't meet the victim, *and* she was overheard by several witnesses earlier in the day wishing for Mandy's death... Plus, the fact that she lied about her alibi makes her look even more suspicious... and me too... Oh God, and I thought I was helping—"

"Whaddya mean? What do you have to do with anything?"

Caitlyn told Pomona the whole story, including her own attempt to cover up for Evie.

"Why didn't the Widow Mags lie too and say Evie returned the vial?" asked Pomona.

"Maybe she would have, if she had known. But Inspector Walsh is a wily old fox. He obviously didn't completely believe me—that's why he double-checked with the Widow Mags. And I'm sure he didn't tell her about Evie's prints being found on the cupboard door—he probably just asked her to go over the events of that night again and, in particular, the details of who returned the vial to the stillroom."

"Oh yeah... classic police technique to see if witness accounts match up," said Pomona gloomily.

Caitlyn groaned. "Yes, and I got caught out. Now it looks like we're hiding something."

"We need to find the real murderer," said Pomona, her face determined.

Caitlyn spread her hands. "How? If it was that simple, the police would have arrested him by now."

"So you're sure it's a 'he'? You think it's one of

those two guys in the village?"

"Yes, my money's on Dennis Kirby," said Caitlyn. "I'm sure he's guilty. He was after the potion, he knew where it was being kept, and he's ruthless enough to do anything… The problem is convincing the police of that! Inspector Walsh just doesn't believe that Kirby could be guilty."

"But he accepts that the guy was at the shop that day and was after something from the Widow Mags, right?"

"Yes, but Kirby insists that he never knew about a magical 'love potion'—he says he was just interested in the Widow Mags's chocolate sauce recipe. And there's nobody to contradict him. Well, except me and Professor Ruskin. Inspector Walsh isn't going to believe anything I say now—and he thinks the professor is completely nuts anyway." Caitlyn sighed in frustration. "But the biggest problem is, Kirby has an alibi. And you know what the police are like about alibis. The fact that Kirby has an alibi and Evie doesn't—and has a better motive, in the inspector's mind—is enough to stack the odds against her."

"What's Kirby's alibi again?"

"He was talking to someone at a cocoa plantation in Indonesia. He used the landline in the pub, so the police have a record of the call—and it shows that Kirby was definitely talking on the phone during the time of the murder."

"Maybe he did it by astral projection," joked

Pomona. "You know, his body stayed in his room talking while his spirit floated out the window and went over to the chocolate shop."

Caitlyn gave a humourless laugh. "Good luck trying to convince Inspector Walsh of that one."

***

Things were very subdued for the rest of the day. Although she told herself that Evie would be fine, that the police wouldn't really be able to charge her with murder, Caitlyn couldn't stop worrying about her young cousin. She and Pomona spent the rest of the day at *Bewitched by Chocolate*, until a tired, worried-looking Bertha arrived late that evening to tell them that Evie would be spending the night in custody. Pomona returned with Bertha to the herbal store, leaving Caitlyn alone with the Widow Mags. The old witch maintained a brooding silence and Caitlyn knew that she was probably blaming herself for Evie's arrest, even though it wasn't really her fault. *If only Evie had told the police the truth from the beginning*, thought Caitlyn. Although since Inspector Walsh seemed so fixated on the teenage grudge theory, she wondered if it would have made any difference. It might simply have convinced him of Evie's guilt even more.

At last, Caitlyn bade her grandmother goodnight and went to bed. She had a restless night and was up again at dawn, lying wide awake, staring at the ceiling. *There has to be a way of changing Inspector Walsh's mind,* she thought. Maybe if she could speak to him again and try to convince him of Kirby's potential as the murderer... but what could she say? How could she argue against a lack of connection to the victim and a rock-solid alibi?

She tossed and turned for another half an hour before finally giving up and deciding to go for an early morning walk. *I'll go and visit Ferdinand,* she thought. Dressing quickly, she crept down to the kitchen and rummaged through the fridge, helping herself to an apple and two sticks of carrots. A few minutes later, she was enjoying the morning sunshine as she took the route from the back of the cottage, across the foot of the hill and towards the fields.

Dew was still sparkling on the grass and the air was sweet and fresh. Birds wheeled in the sky and, somewhere nearby, a blackbird and a robin were having a singing contest. Caitlyn breathed deeply, feeling a sense of calm settle over her. She followed the curve of the village boundary until she came to a familiar field and heard the musical lowing of the cows. The herd was by the fence today and she peered at them hopefully, wondering if Ferdinand might be mingling happily with them at last. But no, there was no sign of the bull.

Then she spotted him, standing alone on the other side of the field, like a naughty child who had been banished to a corner of the class. He had his head down, his ears drooping, and he looked sad and forlorn.

"Ferdinand..." Caitlyn called softly. "Ferdinand...!"

The bull jerked his head up, his big dark eyes brightening at the sight of her. He lumbered up to the fence, mooing joyfully.

"Hello, sweetie..." crooned Caitlyn, reaching out to rub his neck as he thrust his head over the fence and nuzzled her. She looked over at the cows in exasperation. "You poor thing... are they still ignoring you?"

"*MOOOO...*" said Ferdinand mournfully.

"Never mind. Look, I've brought you some treats." Caitlyn fished a carrot out of her pocket and held it out to the bull.

He sniffed it eagerly, his long, fleshy tongue darting out and curling around the carrot. Caitlyn laughed as he drew it into his mouth and crunched loudly. She fed him the other carrot and then the apple. For a moment, there was nothing but the sound of contented munching and she leaned against the fence, absent-mindedly rubbing Ferdinand's neck as he chewed.

Her thoughts drifted back to the murder and she felt the frustration returning. She decided that even though she didn't have any specific arguments, she would go and speak to Inspector Walsh again anyway. *Maybe I should tell him Pomona's theory of astral projection*, she thought with a wry smile, imagining the inspector's face as she tried to explain the idea of Kirby still being on the phone, while also transporting himself to the other side of the village. *Yeah, that would go down really well...*

Then she paused in her stroking. *Wait a minute...* what if Pomona was right? What if Kirby *had* figured out a way to be on the phone while also simultaneously sneaking over to the Widow Mags's cottage? No, not using astral projection—but something much more ingenious!

She gave Ferdinand a final pat, then took a shortcut that led back into the village. She jogged quickly through the narrow, cobbled lanes until she reached the other side of the village where Bertha and Evie's cottage was situated. The shop door wasn't open so she ran around to the rear alley and banged on the back door. After several minutes of frantic knocking, it was finally opened by Pomona, rubbing her eyes and yawning.

"Jeez, Caitlyn, what's with all the racket?"

"Pomona, I've got it! I've figured out how Kirby could have faked his alibi!" Caitlyn peered over her cousin's shoulder. "Is Bertha around?"

"No, she told me last night that she was gonna go to the Manor this morning to speak to James. I think Inspector Walsh was going to be there as well."

"Then we've got to get up there too," said Caitlyn. "Come on! It's the perfect chance for me to speak to the inspector. There's no time to lose."

Pomona yawned again. "All right. Let me get dressed."

Caitlyn waited in an agony of impatience as Pomona showered and got ready, and practically bundled her out of the cottage as soon as she was dressed. A few minutes later, they were driving out of Tillyhenge and heading towards the Manor. Huntingdon Manor was actually located on the other side of the hill behind the Widow Mags's cottage and could be reached in about fifteen minutes on foot if you took the shortcut over the hill—but by car, the only route was to leave the village, join the main road which circled around to the other side of the hill, and drive in through the parklands that surrounded the main estate. It was an annoying, roundabout detour, but it gave Caitlyn time to fill Pomona in on her idea.

"...no one actually *heard* Kirby talking on the phone, right? The police only checked the phone records, which show that the line was engaged. But he could have dialled the number in Indonesia and then, when the other side answered, just put the phone down without hanging up! Then he could sneak out of the pub, go down to the chocolate shop... and then afterwards, return to the pub and end the call. It would give him the perfect alibi!"

"Mmm..." Pomona mused. "You could be on to something..."

Caitlyn gave the other girl a warm smile "It was your suggestion about astral projection that gave me the idea. This is a *non-magical* way for him to be there, on the phone, while also being somewhere else."

"He'd need an accomplice in Indonesia—someone to take the call and not hang up," Pomona pointed out.

"Yes, but the point is: it could be done."

She couldn't wait to tell Inspector Walsh about her theory. Surely, with this suggestion, he would have to take Dennis Kirby seriously as a murder suspect?

CHAPTER TWENTY-THREE

They arrived at the Manor and hurried to the Library, which the police were still using as their temporary Incident Room. But when they arrived, they found a uniformed constable standing guard outside.

"The inspector is in a meeting at the moment," he said, preventing them from entering.

"I've got some really important information for him—to do with the Mandy Harper murder enquiry," Caitlyn said.

"You can talk to me."

"No, I need to speak to Inspector Walsh," Caitlyn insisted.

"Then you'll have to wait, miss. You can take a seat there, if you like, and I'll let him know as soon as he's done." He indicated a window seat across the hallway.

Reluctantly, the two girls went over to the enormous double-hung sash window. It looked out over the landscaped grounds on one side of the Manor, with the rose gardens in the foreground and a wide expanse of lawn beyond. As they sat down on the cushioned window seat, they heard a distant whirring sound, which grew progressively louder.

"It sounds like a helicopter," said Caitlyn.

They leaned towards the windowpane, peering up at the sky. A moment later, they both started in surprise as a large helicopter appeared right over their heads. It must have come from behind the manor house. It was descending now, lowering itself smoothly onto the centre of the lawn, its whirling blades sending a hurricane-like gust of wind around the gardens, causing all the flowers and foliage to whip wildly.

At last the whirling blades slowed and stopped. Caitlyn stared at the sleek black helicopter. It was quite a jarring sight, this monster of technology, sitting in the middle of the manicured lawn, its gleaming black metal body contrasting sharply against the earthy tones and soft pastel hues of the Cotswolds countryside. She wondered who it belonged to and, as if in answer to her question, a hulking, muscular man, who looked more like a nightclub bouncer than a pilot, got out from the front and hurried to the rear compartment. He opened its door and stepped back deferentially as a tall, dark-haired man, dressed all in black, emerged. Caitlyn caught a glimpse of piercing blue eyes in a cruelly handsome face before the man turned away, his long legs taking him quickly across the lawn. In a second, he had disappeared around the corner of the building and vanished from sight, with the pilot hurrying after him.

Next to her, Pomona gave a gasp. "That was Thane Blackmort!"

"The man in black?"

Pomona nodded. "That's why they call him the Black Tycoon. He only ever wears black; he always drinks black vodka and he only travels in his black limo or his black private jet."

"Or his black helicopter," said Caitlyn, nodding at the sleek monster on the lawn. "Likes to make a statement, doesn't he?"

"Omigod, I totally forgot that James mentioned Blackmort was coming for a meeting this morning." Pomona ran a hand through her hair. "Does my hair look okay? Damn, I should have worn my white playsuit—it shows off my tan so much better." She looked at Caitlyn reproachfully. "And you rushed me out before I had time to put on proper make-up—"

Caitlyn raised her eyebrows. "Does it matter? You're not going to see Blackmort anyway."

Pomona cast a quick look at the hallway around them, as if expecting Blackmort to suddenly pop out from behind a pillar. "Well, you never know... I might just happen to 'bump' into him." She grinned and winked at Caitlyn.

She took out a mirror and began fussing with her hair while they sat back on the window seat to wait. It was another fifteen minutes before they finally heard a door open behind them and turned to see the uniformed constable standing in the Library doorway.

"The inspector will see you now," he said.

They followed him into the Library, which looked very different from the last time Caitlyn had seen it. There was now a conference table set up at one end, with a large mobile whiteboard next to it, covered in scribbles. Several archive boxes were stacked on the table, as well as folders, piles of paper, computer cables, two laptops, and various office equipment. Inspector Walsh looked up from reading a report as the constable ushered the girls to the table.

"Ah, Miss Le Fey... you wanted to see me?"

"Yes. I know how Dennis Kirby faked his alibi!" said Caitlyn without preamble and launched straight into her theory.

But he barely listened to half her explanations before he interrupted her. "Before you get too excited, Miss Le Fey, let me tell you that there is no question of arresting Mr Kirby."

Caitlyn drew back. "What do you mean? I don't understand, if he's the murderer then why wouldn't you arrest him—"

"Ah, but that is the whole point. Mr Kirby cannot

have been the murderer because he has a solid alibi."

"But... but that's just what I've been telling you!" Caitlyn spluttered. "He *doesn't* have a solid alibi! It could easily have been faked. Surely you can see that? Like I said, he didn't have to be actually talking on the phone for the line to be engaged the whole time—"

"I'm well aware of that, Miss Le Fey." The inspector glowered at her. "Which is why I have been attempting to locate the recipient of the call and corroborate Kirby's story. I'm pleased to say that I managed to do that this morning—I have since spoken to the cocoa plantation owner myself. He confirmed that he was talking with Dennis Kirby for over forty minutes on the night of Mandy Harper's murder. So, as I said, arresting Mr Kirby is out of the question. Whatever his motives or inclinations, he simply could not have been in two places at the same time. He cannot have been the murderer."

Caitlyn opened her mouth to protest, then shut it again. She hated to admit it, but he was right. She sat back, crestfallen.

"What about Evie?" Pomona spoke up.

"She is still helping us with our enquiries."

"*'Helping you with...'*—that's a nice way of putting it!" snorted Pomona. "You arrested her!"

"Evie is in custody, yes, but she has not been charged with any crime yet," said Inspector Walsh.

"We are still continuing with the investigation."

"You can't hold her without proof," insisted Pomona. "I've watched British cop shows on TV. I know. You gotta charge her with a crime after twenty-four hours or release her."

The inspector's face hardened. "In actual fact, we can apply to hold someone for up to four days in the case of a serious crime like murder. Now, if you'll excuse me, I have a lot of work to do." He stood up and looked pointedly at them.

Caitlyn got up numbly and allowed herself to be led out of the Library. She had thought they were so close to solving the mystery of Mandy Harper's murder—and now it seemed like they were back to square one again. And the clock was ticking for Evie. What if the unthinkable happened and her cousin was charged with the murder?

They walked away from the Library, down the hallway, with Pomona still fuming loudly. As they passed the window seat again, Caitlyn glanced out and noticed that the blades of the helicopter were rotating again. It was preparing to take off.

"Hey, it's leaving already!" cried Pomona in disappointment, hurrying closer to the window and pressing her nose against the glass.

As they watched, the helicopter lifted gracefully from the lawn, turning in an arc so that the sun shone full on its gleaming black belly. Caitlyn caught sight of a strange silver logo emblazoned on its side—a twisting mass of calligraphic strokes which entwined to form the shape of a horse's head. Then it was lifting into the air, higher and higher, before gliding smoothly away from the Manor. It veered in the direction of the hill, hovering for a moment above the stone circle at the top, then continued into the distance, until it was just a speck in the sky.

They heard a step behind them and turned to see a young woman coming swiftly down the hallway, carrying a large tray in her hands. It was Traci, the barmaid who had been helping at dinner the other evening. Once again, she wasn't dressed in the elegant dark colours of the Manor's usual staff—she was wearing jeans and a pretty cardigan with pink glass buttons in the shape of clover leaves, and looked more like she was going out on a lunch date.

"Was that Thane Blackmort?" asked Pomona. "Did he leave already?"

Traci nodded.

"He didn't stay long," said Pomona, pouting.

"Yeah, meetin' were over in two secs. An' me havin' just made tea an' everythin'," grumbled Traci, indicating the tray she was carrying, which contained a full tea service and a platter of shortbread biscuits. "I just took this into Lord Fitzroy's study an' had to take it straight back out again. Not that that Blackmort chap would have probably eaten anythin' anyway—not with that gorilla hoverin' all over him," she added with a scowl. "Some kind of bodyguard, he was—got a bloody cheek, askin' me what was in the biscuits an' saying Mr Blackmort won't touch food not made by his personal chef. I mean, for cryin' out loud, it's only shortbread—not some dodgy prawn cocktail or somethin'—but you'd think it was poisoned, the way he was carryin' on!"

She paused for a breath and glanced at Caitlyn. "What? Why're you starin' at me?"

"N-nothing," mumbled Caitlyn, dropping her gaze. "Sorry, I was just thinking about something..."

"You girls came to see the inspector?" Traci looked at them curiously.

"Yeah, for all the good that did," Pomona muttered under her breath.

"I heard that he made an arrest yesterday?" said Traci, looking pleased. "Bertha's daughter—that weird, skinny girl?"

"Evie's not weird!" Pomona snapped. "She's just very shy."

"They say her mother's a witch," said Traci with a meaningful look.

Pomona hesitated, obviously torn between denying it—which seemed insulting and disrespectful to Bertha—and acknowledging it, which would fuel the village prejudice even more.

"What's that got to do with anything?" she said at last.

Traci shrugged. "Would explain how Mandy died. Word is, she just dropped dead on the spot..." She gave an exaggerated shudder. "That's right creepy, that is."

"She didn't just drop dead," said Caitlyn. "She was pushed. Someone shoved Mandy backwards and she fell over and hit her head on a rock. It fractured her skull and caused bleeding in her brain. It's all in the autopsy reports. There's nothing supernatural or 'creepy' about it."

Traci looked uncomfortable. "Well, Inspector Walsh still thinks it was Evie," she said. "An' I think he's right. Everyone knows Mandy was a right little cow—looked like butter wouldn't melt in her mouth but ready to stick it in you the minute your back was turned. She'd do stuff to you just to watch you squirm. Evie would be just the type for her to pick on. Can't really blame Evie, to be honest, for wantin' to get her own back."

"Evie *didn't* kill Mandy to get back at her," said Caitlyn, her voice rising in frustration. "I know Inspector Walsh believes that but it's not true! Evie could never murder anyone."

Traci shrugged again and said, "Well, the police wouldn't arrest her unless they were sure, right? They must have evidence or somethin'."

"No, they don't—they're just a bunch of morons!" said Pomona with a scowl. "But we're not gonna let them lock up Evie for something she didn't do. We're gonna—"

"Don't go messin' around with stuff that's none of your business," said Traci sharply. "You let the police do their job. Everyone in the village wants the case closed."

"What, even if it means putting an innocent girl in jail?" snarled Pomona, her face getting red. "I can't believe you—"

"Pomona..." Caitlyn put a hand out to restrain her cousin. Part of her wanted to see Pomona lay into the bar maid—Traci's insolent, unsympathetic attitude was getting on her nerves as well—but she'd seen Pomona lose her temper before and it wasn't pretty.

"*Traci!*"

They all turned to see Mrs Pruett standing at the other end of the hallway, her hands on her hips. "What are you doing gossiping there? There's work to do!"

Traci gave them a sour look, then turned and slunk off. A minute later, she and Mrs Pruett had disappeared back to the kitchen. Caitlyn stood looking after them thoughtfully.

"What a cow!" Pomona fumed. "James should fire her! Stupid, sanctimonious—"

"Pomie," said Caitlyn suddenly.

"What?" Pomona paused her tirade.

"I just realised something... Remember that day when we were in Angela's boutique and I went out the back?"

"Yeah?"

"Well, I overheard two women talking. One of them was Angela... and the other one was Traci!"

"How do you know?"

"It was that phrase she used—'dodgy prawn cocktail'—she used it that day as well, when she was telling Angela why she had missed the coven meeting. I recognised her voice. She said it with exactly the same accent."

"Wait a minute, wait a minute... are you telling me that Traci is part of this fake witches' coven thing—but she's also going around dissing Evie for being a witch?" demanded Pomona.

"Well, you said it yourself—they probably don't see what they do as 'real' witchcraft. I'm sure they see it as just harmless fun, whereas they'll say Bertha and the Widow Mags are practising dark magic."

"That's just freaking hypocrisy! We should go back and see Inspector Walsh—"

"And tell him what?" said Caitlyn. "First of all, he probably wouldn't believe us. You know how dismissive he is about anything to do with magic and witchcraft."

"Yeah... and I guess Angela and Traci and the others would probably deny it," Pomona muttered.

"Even if they didn't, it's not like it's a crime, you know. People can dress up and dance around a bonfire, pretending to be witches, if they want to. He'll probably say it's not a matter for the police—not unless they're making enough noise to be considered a 'public nuisance' or something like that."

Pomona's eyes flashed. "Well, at least the next time Traci opens her big fat mouth about Evie's mother being a witch, I'll know what to say!"

CHAPTER TWENTY-FOUR

The encounter with Traci bothered Caitlyn for the rest of the day, although she couldn't understand why. Maybe it was just the barmaid's callous indifference to Evie's plight or her hypocritical attitude towards witchcraft—Pomona certainly fumed and grumbled about that all the way back to Tillyhenge—but Caitlyn felt like there was something else. Something that niggled at the back of her mind...

The chocolate shop was unusually busy that afternoon, which kept Caitlyn occupied. But even as she gladly served the customers and helped the Widow Mags with the chocolate making, she couldn't stop thinking about poor Evie, alone and terrified in a police cell.

She *had* to find the real murderer. It was the

only way to convince Inspector Walsh to release her young cousin—by giving him a better suspect.

But who? thought Caitlyn. With Dennis Kirby out of the picture, the only person left was Professor Ruskin. Could he be a murderer? She thought back to her encounters with the eccentric old academic. Yes, he had seemed amusing and crazy, but perhaps there was a darker side to his obsession with Shakespeare's play. She thought of the manic gleam in his eyes as he talked of being published in top literary journals and making his colleagues regret laughing at him. To return to his old university with a real-life version of the love potion in *A Midsummer Night's Dream* would be the ultimate victory against all those who had scorned his theories.

And he could have been lying about Kirby not telling him the potion's location. If the businessman had been drunk enough to blurt out its existence, he might have just as easily revealed where it was stored. Professor Ruskin could have simply kept quiet about that information. And okay, while Dennis Kirby's alibi may have held, Caitlyn knew that the professor *had* left the pub on the night of the murder. When she overheard Kirby shouting at Professor Ruskin in his room, the businessman had accused the professor of sneaking out after dark. What was it he had said?

"...I saw you from my window as I was talking on the phone. You were scurrying off into the forest, just

after the barmaid went out. Yeah, that's right. You didn't think anyone else saw you, did you? And it was just before midnight—more than enough time for you to get to the chocolate shop and murder that girl."

Yes, if Professor Ruskin had gone into the forest, he would've had an easy, concealed route through the trees from the pub to the chocolate shop.

"Is that whipped cream going to be done any time before Christmas?" growled a voice.

Caitlyn jumped and came back to her surroundings. She was standing at the wooden table in the kitchen, holding a bowl of fresh cream and a whisk in her hands. Pomona was on the other side of the table, carefully cutting up chocolate fudge brownies into chunks (and stealing a few bites as she went) whilst the Widow Mags stood next to her, mixing something in a bowl of her own.

"Sorry," said Caitlyn, bending her head back to the fresh cream. She applied the whisk with great energy and was rewarded a few minutes later with a mound of snowy-white whipped cream, its surface covered in soft peaks.

Caitlyn glanced over at the Widow Mags, who had a bowl of cream cheese, carefully mixed so that there were no more lumps. The old witch was now adding a teaspoon of vanilla extract and a pinch of salt, followed by a generous cup of fresh cream. She whipped the contents of the bowl expertly, until a thick, fluffy, creamy mixture formed.

"What are you making?" asked Pomona.

"Chocolate mousse," said the Widow Mags. "I'm making a Chocolate Fudge Brownie and Raspberry Trifle. It's something new I'm thinking of offering in the shop so I'm just testing the recipe."

"Mm-mm…" said Pomona, eyeing the ingredients appreciatively. "I haven't even tasted it yet but I can tell you already it's going to be a huge hit!"

Caitlyn silently agreed. She could feel her mouth already starting to water as she watched the Widow Mags mix a bowl of rich, melted chocolate into the bowl of cream cheese mix, combining the two until all the mousse turned a beautiful chocolate brown. As the old woman turned away to get a large glass trifle bowl, Pomona couldn't resist sticking a finger in the mousse to taste it. But just as she was about to dab her finger in, the bowl jerked away, out of reach. Pomona frowned and tried again. The bowl avoided her again. Caitlyn laughed. She should have known that even with her back turned, the Widow Mags could use magic to protect her chocolate recipe!

"You'll have to wait," said the old witch, coming back to the table and looking at Pomona with mock sternness.

She set a large glass bowl with a pedestal onto the table and reached towards the tray of brownie chunks, wedging a layer of them at the bottom of the bowl. On top of this, she spooned in a thick layer of chocolate mousse, followed by a scattering of fresh raspberries, their bright red colour glowing like jewels. And then she reached for the bowl of freshly whipped cream that Caitlyn had produced and placed a thick dollop of that on top of the raspberries, smoothing it with the back of a spoon. Then she repeated the whole process again, until multiple layers of chocolate fudge brownies, chocolate mousse, fresh raspberries, and snowy whipped cream could be seen through the clear side of the bowl. Finally, on top of the last layer of whipped cream, she added some chocolate curls in the centre of the mound.

"Omigod..." said Pomona reverently as the Widow Mags pushed the finished trifle into the centre of the table for them to admire.

It did look magnificent. And when the Widow Mags finally let them have some, it tasted even more amazing than it looked—the delicious, chunky, fudgy brownies combining with the rich chocolate mousse, and offset by the tart raspberries and fresh whipped cream.

"I think I've died and gone to heaven..." Pomona mumbled with her mouth full. "Never mind about making this for the shop. I want it all for meeee!"

***

Caitlyn was still mulling over the murder when she went up to bed late that evening. More than anything, she was trying to figure out what was niggling at her, like something stuck between your back teeth that you just couldn't extract. You knew it was there—you could feel it with your tongue—but whenever you tried to pick it out, you just couldn't find it.

Thinking of teeth made her think of Viktor and she realised that she hadn't seen or heard from him in a while. Not since the night of the dinner at Huntingdon Manor, in fact, when she had found his fangs and turned them to chocolate. She smiled at the memory. She wondered if Viktor still had his fangs or if he had lost them again. In spite of her initial misgivings, she had grown very fond of the irascible old vampire. Perhaps she'd try and look for him tomorrow, see if he was all right. He was usually hanging around—literally—at the edge of the forest just behind the Widow Mags's cottage. In fact, she might even ask him about the "witches' coven" up on the hill. Perhaps he had seen something while he was flitting about at night...

Then she paused halfway up the spiral staircase. The thing that had been niggling her... it had something to do with the witches' coven! Yes... something to do with the coven... and Traci... and something she had overheard that day at the back of Angela's boutique. Caitlyn closed her eyes, trying to remember the conversation:

"...we were all wondering where you were. You never turned up last night!"

"Sorry... real sick... stayed in my room all night..."

"You look all okay today."

"...passed real quick... have been somethin' I ate, maybe a dodgy prawn cocktail... anyway... wasn't the real deal... didn't really matter—"

That's it! Caitlyn thought, opening her eyes again. Traci had told Angela that she had missed the coven meeting because she had been ill and had stayed in her room all night... but Dennis Kirby had mentioned that he saw the barmaid going out, just before he saw Professor Ruskin sneaking off into the forest.

Which meant that Traci hadn't stayed in her room all night, like she said. Why had she lied? And if she hadn't gone to the coven meeting, where *had* she gone?

Probably to meet a boyfriend, Caitlyn thought wryly. She gave her head a shake. She was seeing mysteries where there were none. She continued up the stairs and stepped into the attic bedroom. Her open suitcase, propped up in the corner, caught her eye. Despite arriving in Tillyhenge a few weeks ago now, she still hadn't emptied her case and taken the contents out. Clothes that she had tossed haphazardly back into the case after wearing them were now piled in a messy mound. Caitlyn glanced across the room at the antique chest of drawers on the opposite wall. If she was going to remain in

Tillyhenge for a while, it was really time she unpacked properly...

She began taking items out of the case one by one, shaking them out and folding them neatly into piles. Then she carried these across to the chest of drawers and stowed them inside. Thank goodness she didn't have an extensive wardrobe like Pomona, otherwise a small chest of drawers would have never been enough to hold everything.

Caitlyn went back to her empty case, shut it, and stood it upright. Then she turned and looked around the room, checking to see if she had left any clothes out. There was only her old knitted cotton cardigan, draped across the back of the chair next to the bed. It was one of her favourites, in a soft cream, with wooden buttons and deep pockets that you could thrust your hands into. She liked to throw it around her shoulders to ward off the morning chill when she first got out of bed.

Now she picked it up and shook it out, wondering if it was time she gave it a wash. One of the pockets bulged slightly and she put a hand in, wondering what she had left in there. Her fingers encountered something dry and bristly, and she drew out a tiny bouquet of dried herbs and flowers. A warm, spicy fragrance filled the room.

It was the Midsummer herb bouquet that Bertha had given her... She couldn't believe that it was only two days ago when she had been standing in the kitchen with Evie, each of them receiving a tiny, fragrant bundle. She could still hear Bertha's voice...

"A Midsummer bouquet with a protective charm... Carry it with you and it will keep you from harm... Verbena, rosemary, fennel, dog rose, elder, and—most important of all—St. John's wort. Ancient herbs with powerful magic that will protect you and keep you safe."

Caitlyn also remembered the other tradition Bertha had told them about: placing the bouquet under your pillow on Midsummer's Eve, to dream of your future husband. With a start, she realised that *tonight* was Midsummer's Eve. She hesitated, staring down at the tiny bundle in her hands, then, blushing slightly and feeling a mixture of sheepishness and defiance, she reached over and placed it under her pillow.

As she tossed the cardigan back onto the chair, Caitlyn heard a faint *thunk*. Frowning, she lifted the cardigan up again and realised that there must have been something in the other pocket. She thrust her hand in and pulled out a small, sparkling object. It was the pink heart-shaped rhinestone she had found near Mandy Harper's body on the night of the murder. She realised guiltily that she had completely forgotten to hand it in to the police. Turning it over, she noticed that the back of the heart was flat and coated with bits of dried glue. It had obviously been stuck on something and fallen off.

Looking at the heart-shaped piece of glass again, she noticed there was something familiar about it, as if she had seen it before. But she couldn't think of anyone in the village who wore anything decorated with rhinestone hearts...

She turned it over again in her fingers. Then froze. If the shape was rotated, so that the narrow tip of the heart pointed upwards, it looked more like a leaf. Or rather, part of a leaf. A clover leaf—which consisted of three heart-shaped sections.

And she knew someone who had a cardigan with colourful glass buttons shaped like clover leaves. She had seen her wearing it at the Manor earlier today.

Traci.

She hadn't looked closely at the buttons on the barmaid's cardigan but she was willing to bet that one of them was missing a section of its clover leaf. Traci must have been wearing the same cardigan two nights ago when she met Mandy Harper, and a piece of glass rhinestone had come loose in the ensuing struggle—a struggle that had ended in murder...

CHAPTER TWENTY-FIVE

Caitlyn stood clutching the piece of rhinestone in her hand, her heart racing. She knew she had found Mandy Harper's killer. She still wasn't sure what the motive was, what the connection was between Traci and the teenage girl, but she knew instinctively that she was right. This explained why Traci had lied to Angela about her whereabouts on the night of the murder... and also explained why she was so keen for the police to arrest Evie and close the case. With a scapegoat found and the investigation ended, Traci would be safe and her crime never discovered.

Caitlyn wondered bitterly if Traci had sent the "anonymous tip-off" to the police about Mandy bullying Evie at school. It had been a great way to shift the police's attention onto the shy young girl and give the police the kind of motive that would appeal to them.

She would go see Inspector Walsh again first thing tomorrow, Caitlyn decided. Show him the heart-shaped rhinestone and force him to listen to her suspicions about Traci. She blinked and came out of her thoughts as she realised that there was something in the darkness outside. She had been staring blindly out of the window, but now, as she focused, she saw that there was a bright orange glow on the horizon.

A bonfire!

Caitlyn rushed to the window and peered out into the night. Yes, it was there, just like the first night she had arrived in Tillyhenge... and just like two nights ago when she had discovered Mandy Harper's body. Did this mean that Angela and her cronies were meeting at the stone circle again?

There was only one way to find out.

Caitlyn threw the cardigan on, flung open her bedroom door, and raced down the spiral staircase. The kitchen and hallway downstairs were in darkness—the Widow Mags had obviously gone to bed. For a moment, Caitlyn debated waking her grandmother, but she didn't want to waste any more time so she ran straight out of the back door instead. A minute later, she was climbing the hill as fast as she could, her harsh breathing loud in her ears. She was grateful that it hadn't rained recently and that the ground was dry, otherwise she would probably have slipped easily on the muddy slope. Halfway up, she paused for a moment, getting her breath back, and peered up at the top of the hill. From this angle, she could see less than from her bedroom window, but a halo of pale orange was plainly visible against the night sky and, if she strained her ears, she thought she could hear the faint sound of music.

She dropped her gaze back to the sloping ground in front of her and was about to start scrambling up the hill again when she felt a hand clamp down on her shoulder. She gave a yelp, then turned around to see a familiar old man stooped behind her.

"Viktor! You've *got* to stop sneaking up on me like that!"

"I told you, I do not sneak," said the old vampire huffily. "I saw you rushing out of the cottage in the most unbecoming manner for a young lady. Naturally it aroused my curiosity."

"The bonfire, Viktor—" Caitlyn pointed to the top of the hill. "D'you know what it is?"

"Eh?" Viktor frowned, squinting into the distance. "Oh, I have seen that before. It is merely some silly human frolicking."

"What do you mean? How—" Caitlyn broke off as she heard chanting coming from the top of the hill. "C'mon! We've got to see what they're up to!"

She started climbing again, even faster than before, and she could hear Viktor laboriously following her. At last, they approached the crest of the hill and Caitlyn crouched low as she went forwards. She could clearly see a big bonfire in the centre of the stone circle now, its vivid orange flames licking upwards and sending sparks into the night, and around it were the silhouettes of several female figures.

Caitlyn scurried sideways, crab-like, until she took shelter behind a large boulder that was set a little apart from the main group in the circle. She peered around the side of the rock, watching from the shadows. The figures were waving their arms and moving around the bonfire, and she heard female voices talking, interspersed with giggles. They were all dressed in long hooded cloaks in garish shades of velvet, like the kind of thing you'd find in a costume shop, and—Caitlyn's eyes widened—nothing else underneath. Yes, they were completely naked. A few were sitting on a blanket next to a large picnic basket, and two women were trying to toast marshmallows in the bonfire. On the ground around them were various bits of paraphernalia, from red candles to crystal balls, tarot cards to pentacle ornaments, as well as a large fancy portable stereo, which was playing some kind of Far Eastern mystical music. Just beside the fire lay what looked like a bronze goblet, a large bell and a double-edged dagger with a black hilt.

As the women passed in front of the bonfire and the flames illuminated their faces, Caitlyn recognised some of the figures: Angela Skinner, several women from the village, the postmistress... and Traci! She watched as the barmaid waved her arms above her head and shimmied her hips, giggling with the woman next to her, before chanting loudly: "*BLESSED BE!*"

"They're doing witchcraft," Caitlyn whispered.

"That's not witchcraft," Viktor scoffed, watching them with disdain. "They are merely play-acting at being witches. Listen to what they are chanting—what a load of gobbledygook!"

Caitlyn strained her ears to catch the words, then stifled a giggle of her own. They did sound ridiculous, like something children might chant in the playground:

"A witch I am... A witch I be... Abracadabra... Blessed be!"

Then a hush descended around the circle as Angela stepped towards the fire. She picked up the ceremonial dagger, holding it self-consciously and giggling every so often as she looked over her shoulder at the other women. The rest joined their hands in a circle around her and the fire. Angela raised the dagger high above the bonfire and they all began chanting:

"Eko, Eko, Azarak,
Eko, Eko, Zomelak,
Eko, Eko, Cernunnos,
Eko, Eko, Aradia!"

Caitlyn felt Viktor stiffen next to her. "Fools!" he hissed. "What are they doing?"

"What's wrong?" asked Caitlyn. "I thought you said they're just chanting nonsense."

"*That* is not nonsense," said Viktor with a dark look. "That is the start of the Witches' Rune. They have called upon the ancient gods and goddesses..."

Caitlyn turned to watch again. The women were walking around the bonfire in an anti-clockwise direction now, their voices rising in the night:

"Darksome night and shining moon,
East, then South, then West, then North;
Hearken to the Witches' Rune—
Here we come to call ye forth!"

Viktor was becoming more and more agitated, muttering, "No... no..." as he watched them.

Caitlyn looked at the old vampire in puzzlement. "But I thought you said they were just play-acting. They can't do any real magic, so it doesn't matter."

"They may not know what they're doing but that does not mean there isn't still power in those words. Tonight is Midsummer's Eve, a time when the veil between the worlds is thin, and *that* is an ancient incantation with powerful words of magic. It can indeed summon the Ancient Ones—it should only be used with caution and respect!" He drew his breath in sharply as Angela sketched something in the air with the point of the dagger. "Foolish woman!"

"What's she doing?"

"That is an athamé, a witch's tool for directing energy towards a spell, and she is trying to cut a 'door' in the ritual circle… Does she not realise that when one opens a door, one cannot always control who steps through?"

Even as the words left his mouth, there came an eerie cry from the air which made Caitlyn's hair stand on end. The women in the circle flinched and looked around fearfully. Caitlyn searched the night sky but saw nothing. And yet she felt it… something… some ancient power that hovered nearby… The cry came again, a strange echoing sound—like something from the depths of a cavern in another world.

Caitlyn shivered. She glanced back into the circle. Angela was standing by the bonfire, staring nervously at the dagger, which she was now holding at arm's length. The eerie cry came a third time and then the blade on the dagger glowed red.

Angela screamed and flung the dagger away, into the bonfire. Instantly, the flames shot up, fierce and roaring, and Caitlyn gasped as the fire began to change colour. It started with the athamé, which was now in the heart of the flames, burning a fiery azure, and then the rest of the fire flickered and shifted, transforming from vivid orange to sinister blue. The women around the fire screamed and turned to run but it was as if they were caught by an invisible band, unable to escape. They writhed and jerked, trying to free themselves, and the movements looked almost like a strange dance.

It *was* a dance, Caitlyn realised suddenly, as she watched the women begin to move around the circle again. Except that this time, instead of shimmying and swaying of their own accord, they looked like they were being *compelled* to dance. There was no laughter now, no smiles on any faces, as they spun and twisted in a tortuous parody of their earlier partying.

Caitlyn felt a chill as she remembered Professor Ruskin's words the morning she had followed him: those caught in a fairy ring would be forced to dance... until they dropped dead.

CHAPTER TWENTY-SIX

"What's happening to them?" Caitlyn asked in a horrified whisper.

"They have been bewitched by Dark Magic," said Viktor. "This is what becomes of those who play with powers they don't understand."

"Is it... is it like a trance? Can they snap out of it?"

"They are held in thrall until the strength of the magic wanes." Viktor glanced up at the night sky. "The spell will be broken with the first light of dawn."

"But that's hours away!" gasped Caitlyn. "They'll die of exhaustion if they have to dance like that until then! We have to do something!" She stood up and ran towards the stone circle.

"*Wait, Caitlyn!*" Viktor sprang after her, grabbing

her arms. "You cannot enter the circle—otherwise you will be bewitched too!"

"Well… can't I do something to protect myself?" She thought wildly. "Professor Ruskin said if you run around the circle nine times anti-clockwise—"

"Pah! That is a child's notion. A silly superstitious remedy which might work on weaker magic but not this."

"Then… then *you* have to do something, Viktor! You have to save them!"

"I? I cannot resist the thrall of the magic any more than they can. As your guardian uncle, I would risk it, perhaps, to save *you,* but I do not owe those women any duty of protection." He peered at Caitlyn in puzzlement. "In any case, I do not understand why you care so much. They are hardly deserving of your concern. They have not been kind or generous to you since you arrived in Tillyhenge."

"Yes, but… they're still… people. I can't just leave them like that when I might be able to do something to save them!"

Caitlyn looked helplessly back into the circle. The dancing was getting wilder and wilder, the flames burning even fiercer, and the athamé in the centre of the bonfire glowed like a hot coal.

"The dagger—that athamé thing…" said Caitlyn suddenly. "You said it directs magical energy towards the spell, right? I'm sure if I can just remove it from the fire, it should break the bewitchment…" She cast around, then pounced on a broken branch nearby. "Here! If I can just get close enough, I should be able to dislodge the athamé—push it out of the flames."

"I told you, you cannot enter the circle—"

"There must be some magical protection I can use! Come on, Viktor—that's what amulets and talismans and all those things are for, right? Pomona is always going on about them. There must be something which would keep me from harm..." She trailed off, then repeated: "'*Keep me from harm*'... of course, the bouquet!"

"Eh?" Viktor looked at her quizzically.

"The Midsummer bouquet that Bertha made for me! She said it carried a protective charm. It's made of verbena and rosemary and dog rose... and something called St John's wort... and other herbs I can't remember now. But Bertha said they were ancient herbs with powerful magic that will protect you and keep you safe, especially on Midsummer's Eve." Caitlyn caught the old vampire's lapel. "Viktor, listen to me—you've got to go and get it. It's under my pillow in my bedroom at the Widow Mags's cottage. You've got to get it. *Quickly!*"

"Oh... all right," Viktor grumbled.

He turned away from her and Caitlyn saw his shoulders hunch forwards, whilst his arms spread out, stretching and changing shape into dark leathery wings even as his body folded in on itself, shrinking and curving into a furry ball. The next moment, a fuzzy brown fruit bat took to the air, squeaking loudly as it flapped off down the hill, in the direction of the cottage.

Caitlyn watched him for as long as she could but she soon lost sight of the black speck in the darkness. Below her, at the foot of the hill, she could see the Widow Mags's cottage faintly outlined and the bright yellow square of her bedroom window. She was so glad that she had left the light on when she ran out. It would hopefully help to guide Viktor, whose eyesight wasn't good at the best of times.

Hurry... hurry... she pleaded in her head as she paced next to the stone circle. The dancing was becoming even more frenzied now and within the fire, something was stirring. Caitlyn was almost afraid to look. The heart of the flames was darkening and taking on a strange, translucent quality, but what she saw through it was not the other side of the stone circle and the hill beyond. No, it was a dark void from which four figures were emerging. They were galloping horses, she realised—one black, one red, one white, and one a strange, pale green. Their forms were faint, like the barest wisp of smoke, but she wasn't imagining it—she could see them.

Then Caitlyn heard the soft murmur of beating wings, growing louder and louder, and she turned in relief. She looked up just in time to see a fuzzy brown fruit bat emerge from the darkness. It swooped close to her and Caitlyn saw a bundle of dried herbs and flowers in its mouth. She reached up and caught the bouquet just as the bat flew past and dropped it. The little creature made a wide arc to turn around and land, but somehow it miscalculated and flew smack bang into the stone boulder next to her instead.

"Viktor!" cried Caitlyn as the bat bounced off the rock and flopped onto the ground. She crouched down next to it. It was lying on its back, wings outstretched, dazed but otherwise unhurt. "Viktor, are you all right?"

She got a series of grumpy squeaks in reply. Enough to reassure her that the old vampire was all right. Caitlyn stood up again and—holding the bouquet with two hands against her chest—walked towards the stone circle. But when she reached the gap between two of the stones, she hesitated. What if this didn't work? What if she became bewitched as well? She looked down at the tiny bouquet she held in her hands. Could something so small really protect her?

I am a witch, she reminded herself. *I do not fear magic—I can harness it to do my bidding... And magic* will *work if you truly believe in it.*

Taking a deep breath, she stepped into the circle.

CHAPTER TWENTY-SEVEN

It was like stepping into a sauna. The intense heat nearly took her breath away. It wasn't just the normal warmth of a bonfire—no, this was a supernatural heat from the intense blue flames. The thought of going even closer was daunting. *But at least I've not been bewitched*, thought Caitlyn, looking down at herself with a sense of elation. The Midsummer herb bouquet had protected her.

But she didn't know how long the protective magic would last. She had to work quickly. Steeling herself, she stepped between the dancing women and approached the bonfire. The figures of the horses were clearer now, growing larger every moment, and she realised that there were men riding on their backs. But there wasn't time to look or wonder about it—instead, she got as close to the flames as she could and poked the broken branch into the fire, trying to reach the athamé.

Instantly the branch caught fire, the blue flames swarming hungrily up the length of wood and burning her hands.

"Oh!" cried Caitlyn, letting go of the branch and jerking back.

She watched in dismay as the branch was reduced to a charred lump in seconds. What was she going to do now? She looked around but could see nothing long enough to poke into the fire. And without a tool, she had no means of removing the athamé—she didn't have the skill to levitate it or make it disappear or something...

The flames crackled fiercer than ever and Caitlyn felt a wave of despair hit her. What had she been thinking? Viktor had said that this was powerful, ancient magic; she had been crazy to think that she—a rookie witch with fledgling magic skills—could do anything to break the spell. After all, she could barely turn things into chocolate!

Then she caught her breath.

...turn things into chocolate...

Caitlyn looked back at the athamé, her heart beating suddenly with excitement. Okay, so she couldn't move the dagger out of the flames but what if... what if she could change the dagger itself? Turn it into something which would be melted by the heat of the fire...?

It was a crazy, stupid idea, but she had nothing

else. Besides, working chocolate was in her blood. She was descended from a long line of witches who could tap into the ancient magic of *cacao*. Whatever she might have said to the Widow Mags the other night, Caitlyn knew that this was true. *I can do this*, she told herself. *I did it with Viktor's fangs—I changed them into chocolate. This is exactly the same thing.*

Taking a deep breath, she stretched her hands out towards the flames. The waves of heat stung her fingers, making her want to yank her hands back, but she fought the urge. Instead, she shut her eyes and concentrated hard, sending her force of will outwards, towards the dagger in the flames. She imagined it changing, the silver tip darkening into a smooth, glossy brown, which spread up the blade and onto the hilt.

Caitlyn opened her eyes and gasped. There, in the middle of the bonfire, was a perfect replica of the dagger... in creamy milk chocolate! But only for a second. Even as she watched, the tip of the blade bent and began to melt, the hilt warped and softened into a dripping blob, and, a few minutes later, all that was left of the athamé was a puddle of chocolate in the heart of the flames.

Caitlyn looked up. She saw the four horses and their riders fade away as the flames flickered and shrank, changing back into a normal orange colour... until there was nothing more than a harmless, ordinary bonfire in front of her once more. The circle of women collapsed to the ground, like puppets with the strings suddenly cut. Caitlyn looked at them anxiously, but before she could hurry to their sides, she heard hoof beats.

For a second, she thought the vision of the four horses and their riders was back and her heart jerked in panic. Then she saw that something was coming up the hill's opposite side from Huntingdon Manor: another horse and rider—but real this time, not a ghostly vision. As the horse mounted the crest of the hill, its muscles rippling in the light of the flames, she realised that it was Arion, James Fitzroy's grey Percheron stallion—with James himself on the horse's back. Beyond him, the grounds of the Manor and the house itself were flooded with light.

"Caitlyn!"

James flung himself off the stallion and rushed to her side, his face taut with concern. "What happened? Are you all right?"

"I'm... I'm fine," said Caitlyn numbly. "The other women..." She gestured helplessly towards them.

He turned to the circle of women, who were starting to stir, moaning softly. Caitlyn watched as James went around, checking each of them with gentle, expert hands. Finally, he took a walkie-talkie out of his pocket and spoke into it before returning to her side.

"Are they all right?" she asked.

"I think so." He frowned. "They're very dazed, but

I can't see any obvious injuries... John, my stable master, says the police and ambulance are on their way. Here, why don't you come and sit down—"

He reached out to grasp her hands and Caitlyn cried out in pain.

"Oh! I'm sorry. What the—" James stared down at her hands in shock.

Caitlyn cringed as she saw the red, blistered skin. "I'm all right," she said.

"You're not all right. Those are second-degree burns," said James grimly.

He hurried over and grabbed a bottle of water from the picnic basket nearby. Slowly, he poured the whole bottle over her hands. Caitlyn sighed as the cool liquid sloshed over her throbbing skin, instantly lessening the pain.

"You're lucky—the blisters haven't been broken," said James, examining her hands again. He grabbed a couple of napkins from the picnic basket and gently wrapped them around her hands. "Keep them still, try not to rub the burned skin—until we can get you some proper first aid."

He looked around with a puzzled frown. "What happened here? Those women are drenched in sweat, as if they've been running a marathon or something... What were you all doing?"

"Um..." Caitlyn licked dry lips, wondering what to say. James would never believe her, even if she told him the truth. "I guess they were just having a Midsummer's Eve celebration? I happened to see the bonfire from my bedroom window and came up to investigate."

"How did your hands get burnt?"

"Oh... uh... I got a bit too close to the flames by mistake. Stupid of me... Anyway, how come *you*'re here?" she asked to distract him. "I thought you said your bedroom faces the other way and you can't see the hill?"

He raised his eyebrows slightly, as if surprised that she remembered what he had told her the first time they met. Caitlyn blushed and started to say something else but he answered:

"Yes, you're right—I wouldn't have seen the bonfire from my bedroom window. But something spooked the horses in the stables—perhaps they could smell the smoke from the fire—and their whinnying woke me up. I went down to check on them and saw the glow at the top of the hill. Luckily I can ride bareback, so I just jumped on Arion and sped up here."

Caitlyn noticed for the first time that the huge grey stallion was wearing neither saddle nor bridle, only a loose head halter. He was standing at the edge of the circle, stamping nervously and showing the whites of his eyes, obviously still not happy about the proximity of the bonfire.

"I don't understand it, though..." James looked around with a frown again. "The glow I saw—it looked much bigger than something the size of this bonfire. And it was—" He hesitated. "Well, it looked *blue.* I thought maybe vandals or teenage pranksters were up here, messing around the stone circle with floodlights or something…"

Caitlyn didn't know what to say. She was relieved that the walkie-talkie crackled into life at that moment, followed by the sound of distant sirens. Turning, she could see several car headlights cutting through the darkness, heading towards the manor house. Reinforcements had arrived.

After that, it was all a bit of a haze. Paramedics came up the hill on the Manor's two quad bikes and then the women were transported down the hill in batches. Caitlyn herself, however, rode with James, sitting in front of him and clinging to Arion's mane. It reminded her vividly of their first ride together, into the dark of the forest, to rescue Pomona, and just like last time, she couldn't help being incredibly aware of the warmth of his body and the feel of his strong arms around her. She was glad to have the darkness to hide her flushed cheeks.

At the Manor, the women were treated for dehydration and exhaustion, whilst Caitlyn had her hands cleaned and bandaged. The adrenaline was wearing off now and she felt weak and shaky. James brought her a mug of hot, sweet tea, then showed her to a guest bedroom. But as he turned to go, Caitlyn caught his arm.

"James… wait, there's something I must tell you," she said.

"You can tell me in the morning. You need to rest now—"

"No, it's important... about the murder... I know..." She swayed and felt James put a steadying hand under her elbow.

"Whatever it is, I'm sure it can wait until the morning," said James firmly, leading her over to the bed. "You need to sleep now."

Caitlyn tried to protest, but somehow she couldn't seem to find the energy to form the words. In fact, she was so dazed and tired that she didn't even think about being embarrassed as James helped her take off her cardigan, then tucked her into the soft bed. Sinking her head onto the luxurious feather pillow, she closed her eyes, feeling something feather-light brush the side of her cheek just as she drifted off to sleep.

CHAPTER TWENTY-EIGHT

When Caitlyn next opened her eyes, it was late the next morning. She sat up in bed, blinking at the sunlight streaming in through the gaps in the curtains, and wondered for a moment if it had all been a fantastic dream. Had she really seen Angela and Traci and the other village women bewitched by dark magic? Had the bonfire really burned with eerie blue flames? And had she really broken the spell by turning a dagger into milk chocolate?

Caitlyn laughed and shook her head. It seemed ridiculous now in the bright light of day. She must have imagined it—it *had* been Midsummer's Eve after all. Perhaps she had had her own version of *"a Midsummer night's dream"*.

Then she sobered as she remembered where she was. If it had all been a dream, then why was she in a guest bedroom at Huntingdon Manor? And why did her hair smell of smoke and burning herbs? Caitlyn looked down at her bandaged hands and felt a chill as the vision of the four horses in the flames suddenly came back to her.

No, it had not been a dream. She could remember every detail now, including the way the night had ended. She felt her cheeks warming as she thought of how James had tucked her into bed. And that feather-light touch she had felt as she was drifting off to sleep—could that have been his hand brushing her cheek tenderly? Caitlyn felt her blush deepen. Now she really *was* dreaming!

Pushing back the covers, she got out of bed and opened the curtains. But before she could start for the bathroom, there came a knock on the door and Pomona poked her head in.

"Jeez, Caitlyn—I leave you alone for one night and look what you get yourself into!" she said, grinning. She came in, carrying a bundle of clothes and some toiletries. "I brought some stuff for you and I'll help you wash—you're not supposed to get your bandages wet, but I knew you'd be desperate to get the smell of the smoke out of your hair."

Caitlyn was grateful for Pomona's thoughtfulness and submitted happily to her cousin's ministrations. The warmth of the water and the relaxing, massaging strokes of Pomona's hands in her hair almost lulled her back to sleep as she soaked in the bath. It was only when she was dressed and Pomona was towelling her hair dry that she suddenly remembered what she had been trying to tell James the night before.

"Traci! The murder!" she gasped, springing up. "Where's James?" she asked wildly.

"I don't know. Somewhere downstairs. Why?"

"I've got to tell him... the police—!" Caitlyn ran for the door.

"Hey, wait, Caitlyn—I'm not finished!" cried Pomona.

But Caitlyn wasn't listening. She dashed out of the room, running as fast as she could down the hallway and then the sweeping staircase into the main foyer. She stopped short as she nearly collided with James at the bottom.

"Caitlyn!" He grasped her by the shoulders to steady her. "What's the matter?"

"James... the murderer... Traci..." She gulped, panting.

"Whoa..." he said, as if to calm a nervous horse. "Just take your time and tell me slowly."

Caitlyn took a deep breath and tried again. "Traci... She killed Mandy... Traci is the murderer!"

James frowned. "Traci? From the pub?"

"She lied about where she went on the night of the murder. She said she stayed in her room all night because she was sick... but Dennis Kirby saw her sneaking out of the pub just before midnight." She caught his arm. "We've got to tell Inspector Walsh! He's got to question her!"

"He just rang to say that he's on his way here,

actually," said James. "So you can speak to him as soon as he arrives."

"What about Traci? Where is she?"

"She's in hospital, actually," said James. "A few of the women—including Traci—were in quite a bad way and suffering from severe dehydration, so the ambulance took them in last night and they probably won't be discharged until tomorrow." He frowned. "Caitlyn... you told me that the women were just celebrating Midsummer's Eve. Do you know what they were actually doing?"

"Er... not exactly," Caitlyn hedged.

"Because it's very strange... last night, when the paramedics and police spoke to the women, they all kept repeating the same thing. Something about four monster horses coming out of the fire?"

Caitlyn felt a chill run down her spine.

"The paramedics thought they might have all been hallucinating, although it's strange that they should all have the same vision. Perhaps they were burning some kind of hallucinogenic herb?" James looked at her keenly. "Did *you* see anything like what they described?"

Caitlyn wanted to deny it but somehow, with his clear grey eyes looking directly into hers, she couldn't do it.

"Yes," she whispered. "Yes, I saw it. There were four horses: one black, one red, one white, and one pale green, and they each had a rider."

James stared at her.

"But... but the paramedics were probably right and we were just having a mass hallucination," said Caitlyn hastily, seeing his expression. "You don't have to worry—"

"I'm not worried. I'm just... well, surprised and mystified."

"What do you mean?"

"Come with me."

James led the way through the Manor, to a wing that Caitlyn had never been in before. Then, as they rounded a corner and found themselves in a darkened hallway, she suddenly realised where she was. This was the hallway she had stepped into when she had come through the locked door, the day she had rescued Nibs from the window ledge. Now James led her up the same zigzagging staircase to the upper floor and approached the thick wooden door with the heavy metal studs. He took a set of keys out of his pocket and unlocked the door, ushering her inside.

Caitlyn stepped into the hushed, dusty silence. The room looked just as she remembered, with ghostly white sheets covering the furniture and a row of oil portraits along the wall.

"This is the Fitzroy family portrait gallery," said James. "All my ancestors are here." He waved a hand towards them.

"Are you there too?"

"No." He gave a wry smile. "My father wanted me to sit for a portrait but I kept putting him off. In the end, I said I'd only do it when I took the title. Of course, at the time, I didn't expect my father to die so suddenly and for me to have to succeed to the title so soon." He looked up at the wall again. "I suppose I should really honour my promise to my father and do the portrait for him."

"How come this room is all shut up?" asked Caitlyn.

"It was my father's orders. To be honest, I never really liked this room much and there aren't any valuable paintings by any famous masters in here—plus it's so far away from the rest of the house—so when we decided to open up the Manor to the public, I just decided not to bother to include this in the tour. In any case, I'm not sure it would be good for the Manor's image—especially given Tillyhenge's 'spooky' reputation—if the public saw my father's private collection."

Caitlyn looked at him questioningly.

"My father had an obsessive interest with magic and witchcraft," James explained. He gestured to the shrouded furniture. "He had a huge collection of items associated with the occult. Well, he actually inherited most of the collection from his father before him, but he added to it extensively himself."

As he was speaking, he led Caitlyn over to a frame on the far wall. She gasped as she looked up and saw an oil painting depicting four horses galloping across a barren landscape. One was black, one red, one white, and the last a pale, sickly green. Each carried a rider: men with cruel, stern faces, all except the last, the rider of the pale horse, whose face could not be seen because it was covered by a hood. Despite the age of the painting, its colours seemed to glow with a vivid intensity, almost as if the paint was still fresh on the canvas, and the horses looked as if they could leap out of the frame any moment.

"When I heard the description of the women's vision, it immediately made me think of this painting," said James. "I only saw it once when I was a small boy—as I said, I didn't grow up here; my mother preferred to stay in our London townhouse—but my father brought me in here once when I was six. It's such a striking image, it has remained in my memory."

"Who are they?" asked Caitlyn, still staring at the painting.

"They are the Four Horsemen of the Apocalypse: Famine, War, Plague, and Death."

Caitlyn shuddered. James started to say something else but they were interrupted by a knock at the door. They turned to see a police constable standing in the open doorway.

"Excuse me, sir—Inspector Walsh sent me to find you. He's in the foyer waiting."

"Ah, great. Cheers—we'll come right away."

James started for the door. Caitlyn hesitated for a moment. Then with a last troubled look at the painting, she turned and followed him.

CHAPTER TWENTY-NINE

As Caitlyn had expected, Inspector Walsh didn't take the suggestion of Traci being a "new" suspect in the murder enquiry very well. In fact, she got the impression that if it hadn't been for James's presence, the detective wouldn't even have heard her out. As it was, he listened impatiently as she stumbled through her explanation.

"...and it's not just her lying about where she was on the night of the murder. There's also this..." Caitlyn held out the heart-shaped rhinestone.

James and the inspector looked down at it in puzzlement.

"I found that next to Mandy's body on the night of the murder," Caitlyn explained breathlessly. ". I... um... forgot to give it to the police. It was in my cardigan pocket and I only found it again last night. I recognised it—it's part of a clover-shaped button, which I saw on a cardigan that Traci was wearing during the day. I think this piece broke off during the struggle with Mandy." She looked at Inspector Walsh and added urgently, "You've got to question Traci."

He glared at her. "Young lady, you picked up evidence from the crime scene and withheld it from the police!"

Caitlyn ducked her head. "I'm really sorry." She hesitated, not wanting to admit that the real reason was because she had thought it belonged to Evie and was afraid that it would make the police suspect her cousin more. Instead, she said, "I... I didn't mean to... It was in my pocket and I just forgot about it."

"Humph." Inspector Walsh regarded her with narrowed eyes, obviously not believing her.

"So... so you will question Traci?" she asked.

"This new piece of evidence does change the situation somewhat," admitted the inspector. "If Traci can be definitely placed at the scene of the crime, then she would be a strong suspect—although we would still have to establish her motive."

"What about the love potion?" asked Caitlyn. "We know it was snatched out of Mandy's hands. If Traci killed her, then she must be the person who took it—and maybe she still has it. You have to search her room at the pub! If the love potion is found in her possession, then that would be further proof that she was the murderer!"

"I would thank you not to tell the police how to do their jobs, Miss Le Fey," said the inspector testily.

He turned away and made a call to the hospital. A concerned expression appeared on his face and he had a terse conversation before hanging up.

"Is something the matter, Inspector?" asked James.

"It appears that Traci Duff discharged herself a short while ago, against the advice of the doctors. According to the nurses, she seemed in a great hurry to leave."

"Actually, now that I think about it, she did seem to be very perturbed last night, when the police were speaking to her," said James.

"I'll bet she's panicking," came a new voice behind them. They turned to see Pomona coming to join them. "She was, like, so happy yesterday when she thought the police were arresting Evie, but now she's probably sweating it, 'cos you know, the police are gonna do more questioning about what happened on the hill and they might start digging into her movements... I'll bet she's racing back to her room or wherever she's hidden the love potion, to get rid of it. That's what I'd do if I were her."

"Yes," said Caitlyn. "Yes, Pomona's right. I think the first thing Traci would do if she's worried is get rid of the 'evidence' that connects her to Mandy."

"We'll go to the pub now," said James, his voice

authoritative. "We can go in my Range Rover."

Inspector Walsh acquiesced. "I'll follow in the CID car."

***

The pub hadn't quite opened for business yet when they arrived, and they walked in to find Terry, the landlord, polishing glasses as usual, while chatting to a man in a khaki sleeveless vest with multiple pockets, like the kind that fishermen and photographers wore.

"Hullo, James," the man said with a smile, jumping up and holding his hand out.

"Dr Liddell, good to see you," said James, shaking the man's hand. "You haven't come to see Ferdinand again?"

"No, I popped in to see Terry about his old cat, but I've got a vitamin supplement that I want Jeremy to try on the cows." The veterinarian turned to the landlord. "Actually, I'll leave it here—can you give it to Jeremy later? I'd best be off now. A couple of other house calls to make."

He nodded at them all and left the pub. As soon as he was out of earshot, the inspector stepped up to the bar counter and asked the landlord about Traci.

"Traci? Still at the hospital, isn't she?" The landlord shook his head. "What's this I hear about her smoking pot up at the stone circle? Talk's been going all around the village this morning! Can't have that. I'm a sympathetic man, me, but I won't have anyone doing drugs in my pub. The missus was right. She told me that Traci would be trouble but I was soft, see. Thought the girl deserved another chance, seeing as they never found any evidence of her stealing, so I thought—"

The inspector hastily cleared his throat, interrupting the flood of words. "*Ahem.* May we see her room?"

"Sure, sure. She's in the extension bit, last room, by the rear entrance. You tell me if you find any signs of pot in her room, Inspector! I run a clean establishment, me. Like I said to my missus—I'm a sympathetic man but I won't have drugs in my pub. No, don't even like them smokers, though of course, you can't stop 'em—"

They left him still rambling and trooped down the hallway. As they turned the corner and stepped into the extension, however, they saw that the rear door was ajar and there were sounds coming from the room beside the rear entrance. They quickened their steps and arrived at the room to see Traci on her hands and knees, rummaging beneath her mattress. She glanced over her shoulder, eyes widening, then gasped and jumped up, whipping around to face them. Her right hand was thrust behind her back, obviously hiding something, and her face was pale and scared.

"I'll have what you're hiding behind your back,

please, Miss Duff," said the inspector, advancing into the room and holding his hand out.

Traci hesitated, then sullenly handed something to him. Caitlyn peered over his shoulder and felt her pulse quicken as she saw a familiar glass vial.

"That's it!" she said. "That's the love potion!"

"Ooh! Lemme see!" cried Pomona, pushing to get a closer look.

"TRACI!" bellowed a voice behind them. Terry the landlord suddenly stormed into the room. "What are you hiding in there? If I find you've been doing drugs—and me sticking my neck out to give you a job—"

"I'm not! I've got nothin' to do with drugs!" cried Traci.

"Then why are the police after you? Eh?" He shook his fist at her. "I'll not have you dragging my pub through the muck—I run a good, clean establishment here, d'you hear? I won't—"

"Sir—" Inspector Walsh tried to interrupt. "Perhaps you could let me—"

But Terry was in full flow now. "—and if it's not drugs then what's this I hear about you smoking pot up on the hill? Hallucinations and whatnot—"

A look of fear came over Traci's face. "It weren't a hallucination—it were real," she whispered, going even paler. "I saw them. Monster horses in the fire... and I wanted to run... but I couldn't... I couldn't! It were like my arms and legs were not my own anymore... like somebody was keepin' me there, forcin' me to dance—"

"That was *karma*," Pomona suddenly spoke up.

Everyone turned and stared at her in surprise but she kept her eyes on Traci.

"Yeah, that's right—*karma* for what you did to Mandy," she said, taking a menacing step towards the barmaid, who backed away, her eyes huge. "And if you don't confess, it'll keep coming back to haunt you."

"No... no..." Traci moaned. She was starting to hyperventilate. "I don't want... I can't—"

"Then tell us the truth!" shouted Pomona. "Did you kill Mandy?"

The woman crumpled suddenly. "Yes! Yes, I did," she sobbed. "But I didn't mean to! It were an accident!"

There was a stunned silence.

Inspector Walsh stepped forwards. "I think it's time the *police* took over the questioning," he said, giving Pomona and Terry an exasperated look.

The landlord clapped a meaty hand on the inspector's shoulder and said, "Sure, sure! Bit cramped in this room, mind. Come out to the bar—I'll delay opening the pub, no problems. Like to do everything I can to help the police, of course..."

The inspector looked for a moment as if he would argue, then—as Terry started off on another of his rambling tirades—decided that it was the lesser of two evils. A few minutes later, the group was reassembled in the main bar room. The inspector gave Traci the formal police caution, then he leaned against the bar counter whilst the rest of them pulled up chairs and Traci told her story.

"I was just mindin' my own business, you know—goin' to the coven meetin' at the stone circle—an' I just arrived at the bottom of the hill when I saw Mandy harin' out of the Widow Mags's cottage. Ran straight into me. I could tell she was up to no good—probably stealin' again." She looked around at them defiantly. "That's right, it were her that did the stealin' at that other pub, did you know that? She's a right little thief, that girl. She's one of them types that gets a thrill out of nickin' things from shops and such."

Suddenly Caitlyn remembered the day Mandy had come to the chocolate shop and tried to take the chocolates without paying for them.

Inspector Walsh raised his eyebrows. "I shall certainly check our records to see if Mandy has any history of shoplifting."

"I tell you, I saw her with my own eyes! Caught her red-handed. But before I could say anythin', she went and told the landlord, said it were *me* that was doin' the stealin'. 'Course he believed her," Traci said bitterly. "All sweet and innocent she looks, flutterin' her eyelashes... and then there's me, out of a job and my name's mud!"

"So you killed Mandy in revenge?" asked Pomona.

"*Ahem.*" Inspector Walsh gave Pomona an irate

look. "I said, *I'll* ask the questions, if you don't mind."

"It weren't revenge," said Traci. "I told you, it were an accident! I saw Mandy comin' out of the cottage and I knew she had been stealin' and I wasn't goin' to let her get away with it this time—I was goin' to call her out, so that everyone would know what a lyin', thievin' little cow she was! So I stopped her and asked her what she were up to... and she said, 'Nothin'... and I saw she was holdin' something in her hand so I grabbed it and said, 'So what's this then?'... and she tried to grab it back... and then we were sort of pushin' and shovin' each other... and then—I don't know what happened—the next moment, she was sort of fallin' over backwards and then she hit her head and went really still."

Traci drew a shuddering breath, the memory of the horror of that moment reflected in her eyes. "I... I lost the plot... I just legged it out of there as fast as I could." She looked down at her empty hands. "It wasn't until I got back here that I realised I was still holdin' the bottle I'd grabbed from Mandy. I didn't know what to do with it—couldn't think straight, you know? So I just stuck it under my bed and thought I'd deal with it later. Then the next mornin', I heard all the talk going around the village... about this love potion and stuff... and I realised what it was." She swallowed painfully. "I thought if I could just keep quiet and keep it hidden… then when the murder investigation was over and everyone had sort of forgotten about the love potion, I could…"

She trailed off but Caitlyn saw her eyes dart briefly to James. Then she looked pleadingly back at the inspector.

"But I told you, it were an accident! You can't arrest me for murder!"

"Was Mandy still alive when you left her?" asked Inspector Walsh.

Traci couldn't meet his eyes. "Er… I'm not sure… I wasn't really lookin', you know…"

"Was she alive?" repeated the inspector.

Traci gave him an agonised look, then hung her head and muttered, "Yes. She was moanin', sort of…"

"And you just left her there—you didn't think to call an ambulance or report the incident?"

Traci said nothing. But it was obvious that she had decided to abandon Mandy.

"You deliberately left an injured girl to die," said Inspector Walsh harshly. "In my book, you as good as murdered her."

Traci had opened her mouth to protest again but her voice faded away at the look on the inspector's face. There was an uncomfortable silence in the room. Then the door to the pub opened and Jeremy Bottom stepped in. He stopped short as he saw them all gathered around the counter.

"Sorry, am I disturbing—?"

"I'm afraid the pub is closed, Mr Bottom," said the inspector.

"Oh, I'm not here for a drink. I just popped in to pick up something the vet left for me. Saw him just now as he was driving out o' the village." Jeremy glanced at the landlord. "He said he left it with you, Terry?"

Terry nodded at the bar counter. "Over there. Bottle of vitamin supplement for the cows."

"Ah, yes..." Jeremy reached over to the counter. "Cheers."

Giving them another curious look, he left. Caitlyn wondered how quickly the rest of the village would be on the pub doorstep, hoping to find out what was going on. The inspector obviously shared her thoughts because he straightened up and said briskly to Traci:

"Right. Well, I think you'd better accompany me to the station now to make a formal statement... Ah, Jones." He looked up as a police constable stepped into the pub. "Can you take Miss Duff here to the car first? I'll be joining you shortly."

When Traci and the constable had left, Inspector Walsh turned a stern face to Caitlyn. "Miss Le Fey, I have not forgotten that you deliberately lied to cover up for your cousin, Evie, and also withheld evidence from the police. I am not pressing charges this time but be warned—in future, I will not—"

"Is it here? Have you got it?"

They all turned in surprise as a man barrelled

into the pub, flushed and out of breath. It was Dennis Kirby, his eyes bright with excitement.

"Inspector! Inspector, I heard you got the murderer! What about the love potion? Do you have it?" he asked eagerly.

Inspector Walsh rolled his eyes. "Yes, I have the so-called 'love potion'." He waved a dismissive hand towards the glass vial on the counter next to him.

Kirby pounced on it. Caitlyn was about to protest when she saw the frown on the man's face.

"Is this some kind of joke? This says 'Bovine Vitamin Supplement'!" Kirby said in disgust.

"What?" said the inspector, taking the vial from him. "That's odd... I put the vial down on the counter next to me."

Caitlyn gasped. "Oh! The vet must have left his vial on the counter too and Jeremy took the wrong one."

Pomona burst out laughing. "Oh man! The cows are gonna get a huge dose of love potion!"

James looked concerned. "It's a plant extract, isn't it? What if it's toxic to them?"

"Quick! We've got to warn Jeremy!" cried Caitlyn.

She ran out of the pub, followed by James and Pomona, and began making her way to Ferdinand's field. James's long strides soon overtook hers and he arrived at the field first.

"Did you see...? Has Jeremy given the—is he there?" Caitlyn gasped, panting and clutching her side as she arrived at the fence, with Pomona a few paces behind her.

James didn't answer. He was staring into the field and Caitlyn turned to follow his gaze.

Then she saw Ferdinand.

But for once, the bull was not huddled by himself in a lonely corner of the field. Instead, he was standing in the centre, his eyes bright and his tail swishing happily, as all the cows milled around him, nuzzling him and sniffing him affectionately. Beyond them, on the other side of the field, stood Jeremy Bottom, staring open-mouthed with a bucket in one hand and an empty glass vial in the other.

"Blimey! This vitamin supplement stuff really works!" he called out.

Dennis Kirby arrived, huffing and puffing. "Where... where is it?" he demanded. "Where's my love potion?"

Caitlyn laughed. "Er... in the belly of seven cows."

"WHAT?" Kirby turned to look at the field, his face aghast. "What... you mean... my potion... he's given it to the bloody *cows*?" he spluttered. A vein throbbed in his temple and his face was so red that he looked as if he might have a stroke. "What a bloody waste!"

Pomona grinned. "Oh, I don't think Ferdinand would agree."

The bull turned his big, limpid eyes towards them and gave a happy: "*MOOOO!*"

CHAPTER THIRTY

"He's back again."

Caitlyn looked up at Evie on the other side of the counter, then across the chocolate shop to where Professor Ruskin was settling down at his usual table in the corner, a pile of books around him. She poured a generous ladle of rich, hot chocolate into a mug, which she handed across the counter to Evie.

"Here you go. Take this to him and tell him it's on the house." She smiled at Evie's incredulous look. "I think he deserves a special treat after missing out on the love potion, don't you?"

Evie had barely served Professor Ruskin and returned to the counter when two new arrivals appeared in the shop doorway. Caitlyn's heart skipped a beat as James Fitzroy strode in and she heard Evie give a faint squeak as Chris Bottom followed. James was carrying a wicker basket, from which a little black whiskered face was peeking out.

"Special kitten delivery," said James with a smile as he handed the basket over to Caitlyn.

She laughed. "Thanks," she said, bending to look through the bars of the wire door. "Hi there, Nibs! Coming to stay with us for a few days?"

"*Meew!*"

"Hey, Evie—I wanted to tell you, that tonic you gave me was brilliant!" said Chris.

Evie flushed and stammered, "R-really?"

"Yeah, my hay fever's completely cleared up."

"Oh. Um… that's… that's good."

Chris grinned at her. "Yeah, the next time I have any problems, I'll come and let you sort me out!"

Evie looked like she wanted the ground to open and swallow her up. Caitlyn took pity on her and sent her across the room to re-arrange some shelves.

"How are your burns?" asked James, looking down at her hands. His eyes widened in surprise. "They're gone!"

"Yes, Bertha gave me a special herbal salve—it worked like magic," said Caitlyn with a smile.

"That's amazing! It's only been two days since Midsummer's Eve; the paramedics had said it would take two to three weeks to heal."

"I guess I'm lucky… Actually, I've been meaning to thank you again. If you hadn't shown up when you did, I probably wouldn't have got medical attention so quickly. And those other women too."

"No need to thank me," said James. "I'm glad I was there. It was a strange night all around really—the paramedics even found a little fruit bat nearby."

"Fruit bat? Oh God! I forgot! Vikt—" Caitlyn choked off. She covered up with a bout of fake coughing.

"Are you all right?" asked James.

"Yes, fine... um... what did they do with the bat?"

"Well, it seemed a bit dazed. I wondered if it had been affected by the smoke from the bonfire... Anyway, I had one of my stable boys take it to the vet. He's a good man, Liddell. He should take care of the bat."

Oh dear, thought Caitlyn, imagining Viktor in bat form, squeaking grumpily in a cage at the veterinary clinic. The old vampire wasn't going to like that!

"I just wonder what the bat was doing there," mused James. "Fruit bats aren't native to England. You'd only usually see them in zoos. I suppose this one could have escaped... but how did it end up at the stone circle?" He shook his head. "Really, the whole summer solstice has been very strange this year." He turned to leave, then paused and turned back. "Oh, yes, I meant to give you this..."

He held something out to her. Caitlyn looked down and saw that it was the Midsummer herb bouquet, slightly crushed.

"You were holding this when I found you on the hill. I think I must have taken it off you and put it in my pocket. Anyway, I found it later that night when I was going to bed. I put it on my bedside table to give it to you in the morning, but then completely forgot about it." He laughed. "I suppose I should have just chucked it away but it looked like some kind of special arrangement of herbs—I thought I'd better give it back, just in case it was important."

"Thanks," said Caitlyn.

"What is it?"

"Bertha gave it to me," she said absently. "It's a Midsummer herb bouquet. It's supposed to protect you and if you put it under your pillow, you—" She broke off.

"Yes?"

"N-nothing. You're... you're supposed to have... um... unusual dreams," she said lamely.

"Really? Well, now that you mention it... I did have a very vivid dream that night."

"Oh... what was it about?"

"Well, this might sound odd..." James said with a sheepish laugh. He hesitated, then looked at her, his grey eyes twinkling. "I dreamt about you."

FINIS

Don't miss your next wickedly delicious chocolate fix!

Book 4 *in the*
BEWITCHED BY CHOCOLATE Mysteries

COMING SOON!

Sign up to my newsletter to be notified when it is released! Go to: **www.hyhanna.com/newsletter**

ABOUT THE AUTHOR

H.Y. Hanna is an award-winning mystery and suspense writer and the author of the bestselling *Oxford Tearoom Mysteries*. She has also written romantic suspense and sweet romance, as well as a children's middle-grade mystery series. After graduating from Oxford University with a BA in Biological Sciences and a MSt in Social Anthropology, Hsin-Yi tried her hand at a variety of jobs, before returning to her first love: writing.

She worked as a freelance journalist for several years, with articles and short stories published in the UK, Australia and NZ, and has won awards for her novels, poetry, short stories and journalism.

A globe-trotter all her life, Hsin-Yi has lived in a variety of cultures, from Dubai to Auckland, London to New Jersey, but is now happily settled in Perth, Western Australia, with her husband and a rescue kitty named Muesli. You can learn more about her (and the real-life Muesli who inspired the cat character in the story) and her other books at: **www.hyhanna.com**.

Sign up to her newsletter to be notified of new releases, exclusive giveaways and other book news! Go to: **www.hyhanna.com/newsletter**

ACKNOWLEDGMENTS

A big thank you to my wonderful beta readers: Connie Leap, Basma Alwesh and Melanie G. Howe, for providing such helpful and insightful feedback and helping me make this book the best it can be.

And to my amazing husband, as always, who not only gives me constant support and encouragement but is a dab hand at making up spells too!

21796034R00168

Printed in Great Britain
by Amazon